Ghost Takes A Vacation

Carmen Radtke

Contents

Chapter One

Dazzling sunshine made me whip out my sun-shades. But not even the dark lenses could dim the moment.

Could there be anything more breathtaking than the pastel colored palazzi and turquoise waters of Italy, where dashing, toga-clad Romans had sped past in horse-drawn chariots, noble ladies had reclined in the garden of their villas, and even today fast cars, beautiful women and a zest for life ruled every inch of this sun-spoilt country?

"Watch your step." My companion wrinkled her lovely nose. She stared pointedly at the group of scantily dressed women wobbling on high heels who had trouble staying upright as they straggled to the pier.

One of them bumped into me. At the last second I succeeded in dragging my suitcase out of the way.

"Sorry," the woman slurred and traipsed after her friends who, at two in the afternoon, were boozed up and on the brink of happy oblivion - or searching for the next shrub to be sick in.

We'd run into a British Hen party.

This was not the introduction to the old world that I'd intended for Adriana after a sea journey where I'd relegated her to our cabin as much as I could, but surely things would improve.

They did. Our hotel room overlooked one of the many canals Livorno enjoyed. It had a four-poster bed fit for a queen and a sofa that could easily double as a sleeping space for Adriana.

Not that Adriana did much sleeping, if she nodded off at all.

She stood by the window, every single blonde hair on her head perfectly waved and her evening dress as unwrinkled as it had been when we boarded the ocean liner in Boston.

I, on the other hand, could do with a freshen-up. But then I was only your average 32 year old jewelry maker, whereas Adriana Darling was a glamorous beauty whose charms would never fade.

Literally.

She had died in 1929, when she was a decade younger than present day me.

Adriana was my great-great-aunt, and since she had returned from wherever that was about a month ago, she'd become my constant companion and sometime guardian angel.

She'd also turned my whole existence upside down.

A loud meow interrupted my train of thought. On the small balcony, a cat sat and pressed her paws against the French door.

"Let her in," my great-great-aunt said.

I hesitated.

"Please?"

"Only if you make sure she respects the furniture," I said. "My budget doesn't stretch to paying for scratch marks."

"She'll be fine."

I opened the French door, and the cat streaked in and chirruped at my great-great-aunt.

Adriana stroked her, and the cat chirruped louder. Among her other talents, my great-great-aunt is fluent in cat, dog, and whatever other animal she's communicating with.

I might be the only human who can see her, but animals notice her with the same enthusiasm mosquitoes show me. Which is a lot.

She said to our visitor, "Don't worry, my lovely, I'm sure Genie will find something to eat for you."

Genie is me. My full name is Geneviève, thanks to my Francophile mother, but since hardly anyone could pronounce it to her satisfaction, Genie had stuck.

I had my mother to thank for present company. Aimée (born as Amy, but she'd said goodbye to that spelling before the ink on her marriage certificate had dried and she'd left the Unites States behind) had recently remarried after a long widowhood.

While she was enjoying her honeymoon she'd left me in charge of her cat Cleo and the Darling villa in her home town of Cobblewood Cove. There, murder and mayhem had entered my life, and with them, my great-great-aunt.

Ghost and cat had struck up a fast friendship the moment they clapped eyes on each other. My mother had been a little hurt that her cat appeared to prefer my company to hers when she returned, but since she was oblivious to Adriana's presence, I decided to keep quiet about the real reason. Our absence should be enough to repair their bond anyway.

Originally I'd hoped that Aimée would connect with Adriana the same way I did and I could come to some sort of time-share arrangement with looking after the family ghost.

It didn't work that way, though. For whatever reason she'd materialized for me, blood relationship was not the only key. Objects however played a part, which brought us to our two-week stay in Italy.

This wasn't a holiday. Adriana and I were a team on a mission. We had travelled all the way from New England to chase her old belongings, because as far as we were aware, they held the secret to stabilizing and strengthen her in her current form.

The clothes she wore, her jewelry, and an original brick from the Darling villa in Cobblewood Cove, where Adriana had taken both her first and her last breath, all were connected to her peculiar spectral life force.

It had been a stroke of luck when we discovered that her parents had donated some of her clothes back in 1929 to a young woman. Said recipient had gone on from being brainy but not blessed with wealth, to a scholarship in England, a career as a scientist, and marriage to Lord Taverner, a peer of the realm. Among a townhouse in London and a home in Scotland, the Taverners also possessed a villa in Italy.

The second stroke of luck was the fact that the descendants of Lady Taverner had decided to put some of her stuff up for auction, and that I'd already signed up as a jewelry making tutor on a cruise ship. If five days at sea and teaching a bunch of mature ladies and an historian in his forties counted as a cruise. Still, in return I got free board and three meals a day, so who was I to complain?

The dogs traveling with us had lined up to fill the Cleo-shaped hole in Adriana's heart. As a result, we, or rather I, became volunteer dog walkers. I now officially owned a sash naming me most popular crew member.

The voyage also gave us opportunity to work on our communication, and on boundaries. Gone were the days when I'd looked like a crazy person because I was talking to what seemed to everyone else to be thin air. And Adriana now let me sleep in instead of waking me whenever something excited her.

I gazed at her. She and her new feline friend lounged on the sofa. The little tabby yawned at me, curled up into a ball and settled in for a nap.

Adriana played with the fringe of her shawl. She'd been surprisingly quiet since our arrival on Italian soil.

Up to then, I could rely on her enthusiasm for everything new to keep her cheerful and chatty.

That had even been the case when our ship and its human passengers didn't live up to her expectations.

Honestly, I couldn't blame her for being a little disappointed. I'd seen pictures of ocean liners in the late 1920s, and they were as far removed from today's run of the mill ships as were the silk frocks and tails of the era from the spandex and shorts most modern passengers preferred.

After Adriana's initial attempts to join me in every lesson and searching for a handsome man to set me up with, she'd been happy to walk the dogs with me or stay in our cabin and listen to the Jeeves and Wooster novels as audiobooks.

I gave my relative a fond smile. It must have been hard for my vivacious great-great-aunt to restrain herself for my sake during our trip over.

Although she still seemed subdued. Maybe too much so.

"What's up with you?" I asked. I felt the first stirrings of worry.

What if the change in location didn't agree with her, and her recent inactivity had deeper causes?

Adriana had such a strong bond with her birthplace we hadn't considered how a distance of more than 3000 miles might affect her.

I studied her from under my lashes.

Did her skin appear less glowing, her hair less glossy, and her body less real?

I reached for her arm and touched her.

For a heartbeat I could feel the skin contact, which was a good sign.

What was not a good sign, was her lack of response.

Adriana loved to talk, no matter the circumstances, although she also had her merits as a good listener.

"Tell me," I begged her.

She turned away from the window in a slow, languid movement instead of her accustomed whirling. "I wish Belle was here."

My heart sank. Poor Adriana. She and her older sister Belle had been the closest of friends, right until she died.

No wonder she found me wanting as a substitute on her first overseas trip. Being not technically alive didn't help either.

"What would she have wanted you to do?" I asked.

Adriana pondered. A tiny crease appeared on her forehead. "What do people do for fun around here?"

Since I'd read up about Livorno, I had a few ideas. "We could go for a walk on the promenade or explore Little Venice. It's a really old quarter, with lots of small canals, and supposed to have been created by using the same methods the Venetians employed. There's also the ruin of a fortress dating back to the Medici."

I could feel Adriana's eyes glaze over. No ancient ruins then, for her.

I couldn't blame her. I also was a lot more attracted by her time period, although I resisted adopting Adriana's fashion. Her slinky evening dress oozed old Hollywood glamour, which was perfect for her, while jeans and shirts worked for me.

When it came to Genie Darling designs though, they were heavily influenced by the jazz age, Art Deco and Art Nouveau, and I'd planned this trip around museum collections and antique shops.

The cat's eyes fluttered open. Adriana petted her. The tabby shut her eyes in bliss and purred like a Hoover.

"Come on," I said. "It'll be fun. Your first night in Bella Italia."

"What about the cat? She's hungry."

The tabby licked her lips.

"We'll bring home a few treats for her, if she's happy to wait on the balcony."

Although the auction where Lady Taverner's belongings would go under the hammer was to be held in the Tuscan city of Montepulciano, where Milady's grandchildren had done some spring cleaning before putting the house on the market, we wouldn't travel on until tomorrow.

"She says she wants chicken breast."

"Fine with me."

Adriana fussed with her perfectly coiffed hair, and I changed into a fresh pair of jeans.

I watched Adriana closely as we set out. If her languid manner continued, I needed to rethink our plans and head back home with her as soon as I could. I'd never forgive myself if the energy that kept her going fizzled out, forever.

I'd worried unduly. As soon as we were surrounded by palm trees, bars, and the buzz of happy people soaking in the balmy air and beauty all around us, she perked up with every step.

We had barely made it to the promenade, where the black and white checkerboard pavement delighted Adriana so much she skipped from stone to stone, when she froze mid-jump.

Her lips formed a surprised circle.

I had to force myself to breathe. What on earth had happened to her? Would she dematerialize before my very eyes and enter the afterlife or whatever waited at this stage of her existence?

CHAPTER TWO

Someone touched my shoulder. I gave a violent jerk as Adriana landed gently on a white stone.

"I didn't mean to startle you." A broad-shouldered man with an infectious smile, dark eyes and even darker hair, gazed at me with genuine concern.

Adriana batted her eyelashes at him. "Matt," she whispered in unison with me, except that my voice held no tremor, of course.

Matt Blake, art and security expert and the reason we knew about the upcoming sale of Adriana's precious clothes in the first place, had the added distinction to be counted among her favorite men.

His most serious rival for Adriana's affection to date was Cary Grant. She'd fallen for the suave screen legend the second I'd introduced her to "Topper" and the upbeat Hollywood version of a ghostly existence.

I had to admit, Cary Grant in his heydays could also send my heart aflutter once in a while.

For Adriana, watching classic movies with me offered her a glimpse into the near future she'd missed.

For me, they were nostalgic fun and a way to entertain my great-great-aunt. DVDs and audiobooks had proven to be the best way to amuse her without much effort on my side. Those activities also preserved her energy.

After a lot of trial and error we had found out the minimum amount of aids she needed to physically perform a few tasks like drinking a drop of liquid - cappuccino foam was a favorite - or turning the page of an old magazine she used to own. But even dressed in her frock and shawl, with silk opera gloves on and adorned with diamond earrings to give her strength, the effort exhausted her.

Being read to, or having me turn the pages for her, was more to her liking.

Which meant that I got little work on my jewelry designs or my occasional new food blog post done.

Audiobooks were a great compromise, and since we shared a similar taste, I could easily live with listening to Agatha Christie, P. G. Wodehouse, and Dashiell Hammett in the background.

Adriana snapped her fingers at me.

I focused on the man in front of me. "It's great to see you," I said. "But what are you doing here?"

"Looking for you."

"Oh." I stifled a nervous giggle as I watched Adriana go into leading lady mode. She'd decided that I couldn't be trusted when it came to flirting and needed to copy her, to make an impression.

What a pity that Matt couldn't see her making eyes at him in her best Constance Bennett impression. My gorgeous relative tended to identify with the heroines in Cary Grant's movies. Constance, who shared a strong resemblance with her, was her role model du jour.

I kept my expression friendly, in a non-flirty way.

Matt tilted his face a little to catch the evening sun. "It's hard to beat Italy, and this weather."

"Except for France," I said. After all, my mother had named me for the patron saint of Paris, and I'd spent several happy childhood holidays in the country when my dad's work had taken us to Europe for several years.

"True," he said. "But how about we talk about everything over a decent meal?"

Adriana did a little shimmy. "I knew he's sweet on you." She blew him a kiss.

Matt wiped his brow.

She tickled his chin.

I quietly signaled Adriana to cut it out, before the poor man broke into a sweat.

He might not see her, but she did have an effect on him. Whenever she got close, he experienced a warm, fuzzy feeling, which was the only thing convincing me to allow a behavior that otherwise might have come close to harassment. Also, I knew she wouldn't go further than that.

Adriana squeezed in between us as Matt took us further down the palm-lined promenade and into a small alley.

On the balconies, flowerpots with jasmine and honeysuckle released their sweet scent into the air. It mingled with the herby smells of authentic Italian cuisine coming from two restaurants opposite each other.

Both had tables outside on the cobbled pavement, and both attracted a crowd of customers inside and al fresco.

My mouth watered.

Matt moved on, veering into yet another alley. "Does this look okay?"

Adriana beamed at him with something close to proprietorial pride as he stopped outside a trattoria straight out of a movie set.

The terracotta walls had just the right amount of flaking and the wrought iron window bars held just enough patina to prove that they were genuinely old and lived-in. Wine barrels flanked the door and served as menu stands.

"You know your way around Livorno," I said in what must be one of the tritest remarks I'd made in years.

"I could show you around tomorrow morning, if you are free."

The waiter, a slender young Italian with the requisite good looks, led us to a table, handed us menus and lit the candle.

As the setting only offered space for two, Adriana glowered at the unsuspecting man. He shivered, as if hit by a cold breeze.

She smirked. "Serves him right."

I gave her a hard stare.

"Sorry," she said.

Matt gave me a curious glance. Had he noticed my tiny interaction? It couldn't be helped.

"Per favore?" I asked the couple at the table next to us before I took an empty chair. I placed it so I could put my purse including the vital brick on it, making sure I also left space for my great-great-aunt.

"That's better." She wiggled around on the chair. "So, what are we having?"

For someone who couldn't really eat, she took an enormous interest in food and drink.

I'd learned the hard way that she could get tipsy just by taking a deep sniff of wine, and that having a noseful of kale made her burp.

She studied the menu over my shoulder.

I held it so it shielded my face from Matt. That way, Adriana and I could have a cautious discussion about my order without anyone noticing.

Since this dialogue consisted on Adriana making suggestions and me shaking my head in disagreement, Matt chose an inopportune moment to move my menu and hand. He caught my as I just made it clear to Adriana that I would not have oysters, or lobster.

I stopped my head in vigorous mid-shake. "There was a mosquito. In my hair." Another head-shake emphasized my words.

"Stop flicking strands into my face," Adriana hissed.

"Shall I ask for another table? I don't want you to be eaten alive." Matt's tone held a solicitous note but his lips twitched.

I waved his offer off. "The critters find me anywhere. I think the first one sends out invitations to friends and family the second I arrive. But you wanted to ask something else?"

"Only what you'd like to drink. Vino rosso, like the last time we had dinner?"

I mulled this over. As much as I enjoyed a glass of wine with my dinner when eating out, having a soused ghost by my side had its drawbacks.

Adriana twisted herself so we were nose to nose. She practically salivated.

"Sure." To prove that I was not, I repeat not, a pushover, I ordered a mixed salad and vegetable lasagna, in defiance of Adriana's preference for spaghetti carbonara. Considering that she only feasted on the aroma while I did the real eating, she could count herself lucky that I allowed her input at all.

She sighed.

I ignored her. We could dissect my decisions later. The first rule of Ghost Club was, we only chat or act silly when we're alone.

"Smile at him," Adriana said. "Or he might take another woman out the next time."

I felt an unexpected pit in my stomach. Despite my great-great-aunt's romantic notion, as far as I was aware, Matt was only an acquaintance, although one who might be useful when it came to buying back what had once been my great-great-aunt's.

"You still haven't told me why you'd come to look for me," I said. "Or how to find me."

"Easy. The Schuyler sisters told me when you would be arriving. They thought you would like a pre-viewing before the auction." He pulled a face. "Darn. I should have impressed you and said it was my superlative skills of deduction."

"How considerate of them. I'd love a tour of the auction house," I said as the waiter served our first course and filled our glasses.

Primrose and Marigold Schuyler were two lovely septuagenarians who ruled the social register in Cobblewood Cove with a sweet smile and a strict code of etiquette.

They also ran the local museum, which housed items from the slightly less than illustrious history of the town.

Matt had helped me convince them to let me replace items of Darling history which had a connection to Adriana, with other historical stuff.

I'd claimed I wanted them for sentimental reasons, for my mother. If he'd ever doubted my word, he had the decency not to show it.

"To a successful trip." He clinked his glass with mine.

I took a sip and put my glass to the side.

Adriana practically had her nose in it. "That's so good." She sniffed again. And again, like a bloodhound on the trail.

An ecstatic smile spread over her face.

Something had to happen, fast, before she went overboard and became reckless.

The answer to my prayers snuck up from behind in the form of a half-grown kitten. It probably belonged to the restaurant, or at least counted as a regular, because two bowls with meat scraps and water stood next to one of the wine barrels.

Adriana made soft noises and the kitten threw herself at her feet.

"The kitty looks hungry," I said pointedly and arranged the chair with the purse on it so there were no big obstacles in the flightpath between the brick and the food bowl.

We'd figured out that Adriana's independent range from me and the brick covered between five and ten yards.

She took my hint and made her way over, where the kitten meowed at her.

I snapped a picture. Although I could see Adriana as clear as day, the camera only showed the cat and the barrel.

It would still be a nice souvenir from Adriana's first night in Italy.

The kitten kept her entertained long enough for me to enjoy my meal and Matt's company without having to watch over her wine sniffing.

The sunset tinged the sky in ribbons of orange and gold as I put down my fork and Adriana returned without the kitten.

She breathed in the smells from the small bite I'd left for her.

"That was delicious," I said. I stifled a yawn. "Sorry, it's been a long day."

I'd asked the waiter for a little bit of chicken, to take away, and he'd appeared with a few pieces so succulent they might make our new friend renounce ordinary food now and forever.

Matt and I split the surprisingly moderate bill on my insistence. Adriana gave me a questioning glance. I assumed in her days the man always footed the bill.

He said, "If you want to, I'll arrange the viewing and pick you up tomorrow. Is ten okay?"

"Perfect."

The promenade teemed with people as we strolled back. I took most of them to be tourists, judging by the pale skin, ubiquitous shorts, and lack of Italian.

Adriana weaved back and forth to evade them and to admire the glowing ripples of the sea.

For once, she seemed completely lost in the moment, in a good way. I crossed my fingers our good luck would hold.

"Earth to Genie," Matt said.

I realized with a start that he had said something before without it registering. Watching my great-great-aunt while holding a normal conversation was a skill I needed to improve, fast.

"Sorry, what did you just say?" I asked.

"Only that it would be best to have a bidding strategy ready for the items you're interested in. I've seen too many people get carried away in the heat of the moment."

"You mean like a poker-face?" I'd never attended an auction before, so I welcomed any advice, especially since my budget had its limits.

As much as I loved handcrafting my sterling silver and gold plated jewelry, the gems didn't exactly bring in a fortune. Neither did my food blog, although combined they paid my bills.

"We can practice tomorrow," he said.

We lingered outside the hotel. A handshake would be too formal to say goodnight, I decided, whereas a hug might be a bit much. It would only give Adriana the wrong idea.

In the end, I settled on a winning smile. "Thank you for a great evening. I'll see you tomorrow."

The cat waited on the balcony, to be allowed in. The moment I switched on the light in the room, she sat upright, licking her lips before I could do so much as put down my purse.

She guzzled her feast outside, while Adriana perched on the railing and dangled her legs.

I used the opportunity to take a few pictures of the full moon hanging over the terracotta tiled roofs.

Mission or not, I intended to make the most of our stay in Italy.

I had breakfast alone, in the small hotel restaurant. Around me, German, Dutch and American voices rang out. They expressed the usual mix of happiness to find themselves in Italy and the annoyance at the lack of language skills that put most of them at a disadvantage in many shops.

I counted myself lucky that I could get by in several languages, although an adolescence spent in several countries had left me with an accent and vocabulary that was all over the place in my native tongue. I could just as easily pretend to be Canadian, Australian or Irish.

The buffet mollified everyone. Flaky pastries and fresh bread, cheese and cold cuts, fresh fruit as well as scrambled and boiled eggs and thick rashers of bacon tempted me back for a second helping, and the caffé latte made me fuel up with more caffeine than doctors recommended.

I did my best not to worry about my companion upstairs. I'd left Adriana with the audiobook of Agatha Christie's "The Mysterious Affair at Styles" and the brick.

We hadn't been this far apart since leaving Cobblewood Cove. On the ship, our cabin had been right below the room where I taught my students.

I only hoped I hadn't miscalculated the strength of her bonds to material objects. But there was only one way to make sure I could leave her alone at all outside the Darling villa. Otherwise, I had to completely rethink my own existence, and the amount of sacrifices I was willing to make for her to be able to finally live her best life.

When the lift reached the fourth floor where our room was situated, my stomach tied itself in a knot.

What if the experiment had failed? What if she drew most of her strength outside the Darling villa from being with me and not her material belongings?

No. I had to stop being silly. She'd be fine. All I needed to do was enter the room and see for myself.

I paused outside the door straining my ears to hear the audiobook playing.

Nothing.

With a trembling hand, I swiped the key card and rushed inside, stumbling over the chair with the brick.

It crashed to floor, and Adriana let out an anguished cry. "Nooooo."

Chapter Three

Panicking, I dashed to her side. She lounged on the bed, with Captain Hastings narrating in a clipped voice and low volume what had happened on that fateful night at Styles. That's why I hadn't heard it before.

I paused the audiobook and gave Adriana an anxious once-over.

To me, she seemed okay.

Every inch of her resembled a Golden Age movie star, from her hair to the hem of her silk evening gown and the straps of her matching dance shoes.

Everything, except her face. Instead of showing her usual vivacity, she flinched in agony.

"Was I gone too long? Do you feel faint?" The knot in my stomach tightened.

She clutched her chest. "It hurt. When you smashed the brick, it was like a knife stabbing me."

The brick?

She was right. A small corner had chipped off when it hit the ground.

I examined the floor. No damage there to be added to my bill, luckily.

Carefully, I put the corner piece back where it belonged. Adriana relaxed. "That's better. I haven't felt that jingle-brained since that pal at the *Russian Embassy* tried to slip me and my girlfriend a Mickey Finn. One sip, and it was just like this. If the bartender hadn't snatched that drink from me and laid the pal out, anything might have happened."

"But you feel okay now?" I worried. These days, she only sounded like a 1920's gangster moll straight out of her old crime fiction magazines when she was rattled.

I searched my suitcase for the small tube of superglue I always carried for emergencies. I'd learned my lesson when I had to limp for half a mile because of a broken heel.

Superglue, a bottle of nail polish, and something to use a makeshift hammer were among a woman's best friends.

Adriana dangled a limp hand from the bed. I grabbed her gloves and cigarette holder and laid them next to her. Because Adriana only wore or held them in a metaphorical sense, it could be baffling in the beginning to see the gloves on her and at the same time, in their physical form where I put them.

"I'm dandy." She sat up. "You better hurry before Matt turns up. You don't want to frighten off the only sheikh in our life."

I hotfooted it to the bathroom, to slick on some lipstick and mascara and run the brush through my hair, in the hope to satisfy Adriana's expectations.

I didn't want to disappoint or embarrass her in front of Matt. The classification as sheikh was the biggest compliment she could pay a man. I'd fallen below her standards a couple of times, until she accepted that she had exchanged the year 1929 for an era with less glamour and much better travel opportunities.

My new jeans had found her approval though, and as a writer who'd once aspired to become a second Dorothy Parker, she also gave me the thumbs up for wearing slogan tee shirts, if they carried a witty, feminist message. The latter I'd reluctantly left back home. For the work on the ocean liner and sightseeing in Italy though I'd opted for less eye-catching and more traditional looks.

I couldn't blame Adriana for oozing style, even if I wanted to. Her dress, which hugged her body in all the right places, had been the last frock she put in before the accident that had ultimately resulted in her death.

If it had been an accident.

Together we had solved murder cases, both present and past ones. Yet over her own demise still hung a question mark. When Adriana came into my life, her favourite necklace was missing - a valuable item she always wore.

I'd never told her, but I had little doubt that if we would find that particular piece of jewelry, we would discover the truth about Adriana's death, and the reason why she'd come back as a ghost.

True to his word, Matt arrived on the dot in the hotel lobby. Adriana sashayed to the revolving door and propped herself up on the folding seat attached to the sides.

I followed at a more sedate pace.

"Hurry," she sang out. "Last one's a loser."

I give her a tiny shrug and gestured to Matt to go ahead. There was space enough for two people to go together in one compartment, but only just.

Outside, I paused and pretended to tie my shoelace while Adriana spun around and around in the revolving door. I'd never seen anyone living more in the moment. After ten rounds, she had enough and joined me.

A pekingese wagged his tail at her, as his owner strolled past with him.

"Prego, signorina."

The doorman of the five star hotel next to ours held open the door of an all-electric BMW.

I gave a start, until I realized he only wanted me to move out of the way and let an expensive-looking blonde beauty with a mini leather dress and killer heels drape herself into the passenger seat.

A man in a bespoke suit and an enormous signet ring on his pinkie, took the steering wheel and careened away from the curb before reversing at speed.

"Will you look at that car," Adriana marveled. "Ten gets you one that he and his dame --"

She stopped mid sentence and yelled a warning as she shooed the Pekingese out of the way, just before the BMW could hit it.

I closed my eyes, unable to watch, until not knowing what was going own was even worse.

The dog owner rushed to her pet who shook himself in a daze. She clutched him with one hand and shook the other at the BMW driver who sped away without so much as a quick stop or apology.

Adriana petted the dog. He licked her hand.

Matt approached the owner. "Is your dog okay?"

The woman nodded, followed by a slight slump in her shoulders.

Matt snapped his fingers and the doorman of the hotel came running. "Please look after the lady," Matt ordered.

She gave him a grateful smile that tightened a little when she noticed me.

"He really is a great guy," Adriana said with a hint of smugness in her voice as we moved on. "Not like that rich oaf. He'd better not cross my path again or I'll show him. He could have killed the sweet puppy."

I couldn't agree more.

Matt offered to hail a taxi, but I declined. I loved exploring new places on foot, and Livorno was compact enough to make it easy to enjoy a stroll along the canals.

The tall buildings were crisscrossed with washing lines. A grey-haired man leant dangerously far over his Juliet balcony to peg up shirts.

A seagull ha-ha'd as it sailed past, over the grey head. Whatever else the bird did, it was enough to make the man drop the shirt he was holding.

The garment landed on Adriana's head.

I snatched it with a speed that made me proud, but not fast enough.

Matt rubbed his eyes as if doubting his vision. "Did that shirt float in the air?"

My laugh trilled in my ears with all the skill of a dropout from a third rate drama class. "Of course not. It's the breeze catching on things."

To prove my point, I let a clean Kleenex fall onto Adriana's hand. I picked it up as soon as it settled on a limb only I could see. "See? Same thing happened here."

I arranged the shirt over an oleander shrub and mimed to the owner where it was. This trip as a trio maybe wasn't the best idea after all.

"Look at those boats." Adriana tugged at my sleeve.

"How about a ride on the water? After all this is Little Venice, even if they don't seem to have gondolas," I said to Matt.

We selected a wooden motorboat - not the fanciest vessel, but also not the worst.

The pilot had the distinction of wearing a striped tee with a black dog printed on his back. He took us along the placid water under arched bridges and alongside private jetties.

The wind ruffled my hair, Adriana gazed around in rapt wonderment, and Matt pointed out the same landmarks the pilot mentioned.

I relaxed in the golden glow of the sun. This turned out okay after all. I hung a hand overboard, to catch some of the spray.

Soon enough we'd be in the Tuscan hills, so I intended to make the most of my time by the sea.

"Can you stop the boat?" Adriana jumped up.

I jumped up, too. Was there anything wrong?

"Now." She shifted her weight and eyed the pier.

I gave in. "Can we please cut the engine, Matt?"

Matt and the pilot shared a shrug that said a lot about their familiarity with unpredictable female whims.

If I'd been on my own, I'd have told them a thing or two about patronizing behavior and what they could do with that attitude. But I had more important business to take care of.

Adriana hopped off before we'd come to a full halt.

She stepped daintily over a gap that should be impossible even for someone with long legs like hers.

Matt followed. He reached for my hand and hauled me onto dry land.

Before I could think twice, he took my purse. "That's heavy," he said. "What do you carry in it, gold bullion?"

If only. "Just this and that," I said. "Including a brick. It makes a great self-defense weapon." Considering that Matt had been around when I fought off a killer, that explanation actually made sense to him.

I insisted on paying the boat pilot. It had been my idea, and I didn't want Matt to get the wrong impression about my interest in him.

Adriana sniffed the air like a hound dog. "We're close," she whispered.

"To what?"

She ignored my question, although I knew she possessed much keener hearing than I did, so even my low voice should have been audible to her.

Instead, she moved her head this way and that and led us to an antiques store, called "Yesterday's Treasures".

Underneath the large gold lettering on the plate glass window stood the Italian translation in much smaller letters.

"I can feel it," she said.

I pressed the door handle, without success.

There were no posted opening hours, but that didn't matter. I'd found out the hard way ages ago that time had not much meaning in Italy, and was treated more as a suggestion than a fixed thing.

"Closed for lunch, I assume," Matt said. "But what are we doing here?"

That was the question. I couldn't very well claim to have spotted the shop from the canal, because we were two alleys away from the water here.

"Restrooms. I had too much coffee, and I thought I saw a sign pointing this way."

By now, Matt had to seriously doubt my mental stability.

The shop owner saved my face.

While I still racked my brain over my next move and Adriana didn't help because she now hopped on one foot and grimaced like a woman in need of a toilet, giving me another acting lesson, this wonderful woman yanked the door open and beckoned me inside.

At the back I spotted a small bathroom.

"You can use it," she told me in a distinctively American voice.

"Thank you." I hurried inside, my purse pressed to my chest. "What now?" I asked Adriana in as low a voice as I could muster. The kind shop owner must have super-sonic hearing if she could gauge correctly what Matt and I had talked about.

Or maybe she was used to tourists coming in to use her facilities and afterwards feeling compelled to browse and buy. Anyway, I intended not to take any risks of being caught muttering to myself.

Adriana closed her eyes. An ethereal shimmer spread over her face. "Follow me."

For good measure, I washed my hands and slathered them generously in orange blossom lotion provided in a dispenser I guessed to be from the 1960s.

The container was pretty, but not so special the woman could sell it for a good price.

The same could not be said for most of the merchandise.

I fawned over a striped hat box and a set of hair pins dating back to the 1930s. If I had any money left after the auction, I had to come back here.

Or maybe not.

Adriana had located the object of her desire, which made my heart beat faster until I saw the price tag.

The vanity case I was looking at would be mine for 400 Euros.

"You've got a good eye," the shop owner said. She'd perfected the trick of sounding reassuring without being pushy. Her appearance struck the same balance.

I took her to be in her early 40s, with a casual elegance that made her look both accessible and classy.

Adriana gave a modest shrug. "It is beautiful, but so are most of my things."

They were both right. The rectangular case was a bit larger than my hand and made of blue and gold enamel, with shell shapes in the corners. One of the shells was cracked, and a little piece of enamel was missing.

I pointed out those flaws.

"It's why it's so cheap." The woman flicked a soft cloth over it.

"If you take out the compartment, there should be a mirror, with a small chip, if you want to be fussy," Adriana said.

I followed her instructions. She was right.

There were also her initials on the lid, even if I had doubted that this necessaire, as my mother would have called it, had once belonged to Adriana Darling.

Which meant I had no choice but to buy it.

I spied Matt outside, basking in the sunshine.

The show owner inspected the vanity case again when I pointed out the damage to the mirror. "I could let you have it for 350 Euros."

"Where did you get it?" Maybe she had more of Adriana's things.

The woman gave me an enigmatic smile. "I have my sources. This case has already seen some interest from my regular customers."

Adriana glowered at me. "Why are you dragging your feet?"

"300 Euros, and I'll take it," I said.

"You strike a hard bargain." The woman handed me the vanity case.

I pulled out my credit card.

Adriana floated in the air as we left the shop.

I could measure her excitement by the distance between her feet and the ground. Right now, she was halfway between satisfied and ecstatic.

"Goody, goody, goody," she said. "Now let me have it."

I answered with a tiny shake of my head.

There were things a woman and her ghost had to do alone, like letting Adriana take in the essence of the object.

Having Matt hanging around while she did that did not feature in my plans.

So, under the pretext of having forgotten something in my hotel room, I dropped off my great-great-aunt and her new, or rather old, possession.

Matt and I ambled along medieval churches with slender spires, mosaic payments and small cafés with tables under awnings. Sometimes it took a close look to figure out where one establishment ended and the other begun.

We paused for bottled water and tramezzini, thin, hand-cut sandwiches that were a staple of Italian lunches.

The main meal would come in the evening.

"Where are you off to next?" I asked as we moved on. "More jobs here in Europe or are you heading back home?"

Since Matt worked for a private company specializing in museum security, he rarely stayed in one place for long. His home base was close to Cobblewood Cove, but he hadn't been there in weeks. Not that I'd kept track of his whereabouts.

"That depends," he said. "If nothing crops up, I'm going to have a bit of a holiday here. It would be a shame to rush off again without some Italian rest and relaxation." His smile crinkled his eyes. "How about you?"

"Same here. I thought I'll play it by ear." I was scheduled to return in two weeks, again working my way home by giving classes, but I'd done this before and the agency had always been flexible.

A lemon-colored Vespa sputtered past us.

"Very *Roman Holiday*," I said.

Half a dozen more Vespas in all shades of reds, blues, greens and cream followed, making us squeeze into an archway.

The effect had something of a travel poster, although it would have taken more imagination than I could muster, to picture Audrey Hepburn and Gregory Peck riding the sleek machines in the classic movie.

Instead, even in a land as dedicated to elegance as Italy, most of the mature riders had long given up fashion for the comfort of shorts and loose shirts.

At least there were as many women as men among them, something that counted in their favor.

My gaze followed them as they navigated the obstacles posed by narrow streets and crowded pavements.

Matt's thoughts traveled along similar paths. "It makes me feel like I've landed in an impossibly romantic movie set."

"It does."

His phone pinged. He grimaced. "We'd better get ourselves in gear if you want to have a leisurely look at the auction objects. It's easily a two hour drive."

That meant we had to pick up Adriana and my luggage.

"Five minutes in my room and I'll be ready." I prepared myself for the inevitable joking about how women always said that.

I was wrong.

Matt simply nodded.

Adriana got it right. He really had proven himself to be a sheikh.

The drive took us along winding roads deeper and deeper into the Italian heartland.

Cypresses stood sentinel along driveways leading to the farmhouses dotting the hills.

Pines cast welcome shade across the roads, and the fields were as green and golden as an impressionist painting.

My fingers itched to sketch them. I wasn't good with watercolors, or anything else apart from faces and jewelry designs, but this landscape made me feel like giving it a try.

Matt braked as a pheasant with a death wish ran across the road.

Adriana flung herself between me and the door, as vigilant as ever in her role as my self-appointed bodyguard. Otherwise she kept quiet, with her hands stroking the vanity case.

She'd grown in physical substance since the purchase.

Case in point was the change in my seating position when she moved to protect me from any impact. She'd pushed me aside a couple of inches, without her losing any of her glow.

That was worth remembering.

The deeper her emotional connection to an object was, the more impact it had on her. So, if we had to choose at the auction, it would make sense to keep a ranked list.

Another thing I had learnt since our arrival in Italy was that having Matt around had its advantages, but it drove me crazy to keep my tongue in check when Adriana was around.

Montepulciano charmed me at first sight. Like most Tuscan towns it stood high up on a hill, surrounded by massive medieval walls dotted with city gates. Steep, narrow streets lined with tall buildings offered shade.

In the distance, Lake Trasimeno shimmered blue under the clear sky.

Matt drove on, until we reached a stone-walled building with a large courtyard filled with half a dozen cars.

Although the old quarters were only a fifteen minute walk away, the house had the distinction of being detached and surrounded by lawn. On the other side of the road were a few shops and a corner bar, with upper floors probably turned into living quarters.

A wiry Italian with a bushy moustache and a footman's uniform at odds with the tattooed madonna on his hand let us in.

As an avid fan of *Antiques Roadshow* and similar programs, I'd expected a room filled with all kinds of pieces crammed together in a charmingly haphazard way. Instead, this place had more in common with a small museum.

I craned my neck to admire the vaulted ceiling with its faded mural depicting a pastoral scene. Along the walls, numbered objects were placed in vitrines and on wooden mannequins.

Matt gave me a high gloss brochure with pictures and known or assumed provenance.

It also showed the reserve prices.

I read and gulped. For an unknown house in a small town, this came as an unwelcome surprise.

I crossed my fingers that Adriana once was the owner of some of the cheaper items, like a silver backed mirror or the Art Deco headband, made of green and gold beads, circa 1927.

"It's here." Adriana hugged a mannequin wearing an evening gown. "Isn't it a beauty? Belle brought it back for me from Europe."

I stared at the dress. Almost a century later, every inch of the floor length black satin draped itself effortlessly around the wooden doll. The low cut back was held by thin criss-crossed straps.

Adriana inspected it closely. "Would you clap your eyeballs on this! Somebody has made a tear in the front. It's not too bad but honestly, how could they?" Any second, I expected steam to curl out of her ears.

I flicked through the brochure, hoping with all my heart that there would be more objects carrying the words "From the estate of Lady Taverner".

I struck gold in the penultimate page. "There should be an enameled powder compact and a hat from ..."

"Chanel."

Chapter Four

A cloud of two perfumes fighting an olfactory war clogged my nose, as two female voices overlapped.

Apart from a fondness for powerful scent, they had another thing in common - a burning desire for Adriana's dress.

I gulped. This couldn't happen. My bank account couldn't afford competition for a little black dress created by the most famous designer of the 20th century.

Who were these people?

As covertly as possible I studied the two women.

One was a blonde with the exquisite shades created by expensive colorists, and the other was raven-haired.

I instantly wished I had ignored them, and not simply because my nose struggled with the mixed orange blossom, rose, musk and vanilla notes.

They both screamed money, from the top of their coiffed heads to the red soles of their Louboutins.

Worse still, they both had Adriana's height and slender frame. The garment would fit them like a glove.

No doubt they already envisaged themselves swanning down somewhere in a dress that, without the tear and a few frayed fibers at the hem, would have been in a museum.

Adriana scanned them too. "Shoo," she hissed as she glared daggers at the blonde woman, who probably was a little older than me, although much better looked after.

I assumed she had a standing appointment at every pampering place under the sun.

Strange. I'd rarely seen my sunny-natured great-great-aunt in such a state, or have her react so badly to an innocent questioning look from me.

"Open your eyes." Now she hissed at me. "It's the same broad and her money-bags who almost hit that poor puppy. How could you forget?"

She was right. In my defense, the woman had changed into another dress, and I had other things on my mind,. Without the man who strode across the room as if he owned the place, I would still have been unable to identify her.

But he was unmistakable, with his signet ring on the left pinkie and the same stiff quiff.

His breast pocket bulged with a silver case for small cigars.

Adriana blew out what counted as her breath in the woman's face, making her flinch and back off a step or two.

"That'll teach her," my companion said. "That dress is mine. It's special, and I wouldn't advise anyone to go near it, or they'll find out how sore I can get."

Sure enough, she clenched her fists and raised them shoulder high as the raven-haired woman came within two feet of the Chanel dress.

The woman practically salivated as she told her husband, "This little beauty wasn't here the last time we came by."

Up close, I spotted faint wrinkles on her hands and throat. There were some battles with age that not even surgery could help her win.

Adriana danced from one foot to another and feigned a right hook. "Go away, unless you want to hear some chin music."

"Come on," I said through closed lips.

A belligerent ghost was the last thing I needed.

I could sense a stomach ache coming. I kept antacids in my purse for this occasion, but I needed water to swallow them.

Adriana gave her rivals for the frock a last disdainful gesture before she followed me to the far end of the room.

Under normal circumstances I'd have stopped to admire the items on view. They included an original Wedgwood tea set with only one cup missing, and two exquisite miniature eye paintings, set in gold and worn as pendants on a necklace.

I'd read about these things that had briefly been in fashion over two hundred years ago, but never seen them.

These two were probably the most expensive auction pieces in the house, Chanel or no Chanel. If the catalog was to be believed, the miniatures showed the eyes of Emperor Napoleon Bonaparte and his beloved Josephine.

Adriana peered into every vitrine. The corners of her mouth turned downwards. "There's nothing here. I can feel it."

"Not even the powder compact?" With a reserve price of 100 Euro, I should easily be able to fend off competition for that item.

She shook her head. "Only the dress."

"Right. I'll still try to buy Lady Taverner's other things for the Schuylers."

Those two lovely ladies whom I'd adopt as surrogate grandmothers in a heartbeat, had asked me to bring back some loot for the museum, if I could wrangle it.

After all Her Ladyship, who had started out as poor Betsy Grant from Cobblewood Cove, had become its most prominent citizen. Or would have had, had anyone known of her claim to fame closer to her time.

Betsy's ascendance to a title and the so im-portant donations from Adriana's parents after my great-great-aunt's untimely demise had only recently come to the Schuylers' attention.

A man cleared his throat.

I shut up and motioned to Adriana to do the same, so I would neither be caught mumbling to myself nor give away my plans for the bidding.

I'd heard people move to and fro in the background, but only vaguely.

It would be better to start paying attention to my surroundings.

That included the return of Matt.

He'd been conversing in a corner with a dashing gen-tleman in his early fifties, who could pull off combining a grey silk scarf wound around his neck with a pair of jeans and loafers.

Worry lines creased the man's otherwise well-kept face that wouldn't have looked out of place in a maga-zine.

When he saw me glancing at him, his expression changed into a twinkle.

"Have you found anything to your liking?" he asked in a pleasant baritone and with the clipped consonants of an upper-class Brit.

I smiled back. "How about yourself?"

He chuckled, and so did Matt. "That would be a little inappropriate. I'm Tristan Odell, the owner of Palazzo

Vecchio." He gave a little shrug. "Old Mansion isn't the greatest name, but it felt wrong to change it after more than two centuries."

"Genie Darling, and you're right about keeping tradition." We shook hands just long enough for me to feel valued, but not so long to get the impression he wanted to hit on me.

Odell was definitely a smooth operator.

Adriana moved away a little.

I appreciated that. It made it easier for me to hold a decent conversation.

If she intended to spook the hazardous driver and his wife a little, so be it.

"This is an incredible selection you have here," I said.

"Not too shabby, if I say so myself. The perks of being able to offer little competition and multicultural understanding." Odell's voice unsurprisingly held no trace of an Italian accent, but he talked with his hands a lot more than the average Anglo-Saxon.

I assumed he'd been living la dolce vita under the Tuscan sun for a while.

"Odell's is building a stellar reputation," Matt said.

"I'm working on it." Our host twinkled again and turned to the raven-haired woman and her partner, a heavy-set man who would have been unmemorable without her, except for his strong tobacco-scented aftershave.

Odell bent over her hand and air-kissed it. "How nice to see you, Mrs and Mr Stone."

"Our pleasure." Mr Stone hugged his wife to him.

I grinned to myself. Despite the polite words, I sensed a chip on Stone's shoulder.

He definitely had a lot rougher edges than the suave Englishman.

"Fellow Americans, right?" Matt introduced himself to the round, although he gave no further information than his name.

"Got it in one." Stone relaxed. "Although my wife and me have been on the road for so long, you could call us honorary Europeans. We're collectors, you see."

"Sellers, too." Odell pointed to the open page in my catalog.

I goggled. Those two owned the eye miniatures, which meant they had deep pockets.

Blast. If wealthy Mrs Stone had her heart set on the Chanel frock, I stood no chance.

I was still pondering this unpleasant revelation, when loud screams erupted.

The next thing I knew, Adriana clung to my neck, and the uniformed man was dragged past us. He was clutching the arms of a pair of angry, and strong, young men who resisted his attempts to stop them in their tracks.

Chapter Five

"Either you return the statuette to its rightful owners, or you'll have to face the consequences, you thief." The taller of the men spat at Odell's feet. He used his free hand to smooth back curly hair.

His sidekick, a stocky guy who'd soon be bald judging by the thinning patch on his head, swatted at the uniformed man. "Don't touch me."

Odell motioned to his employee to step aside.

"Are you leaving of your own accord or do I have to call the police, again?" he asked.

The two intruders paused.

The taller one drew himself up to his full height. "You haven't heard the last of this."

He made a sweeping gesture that encompassed us all. His gaze flickered over us, changing from contempt for Odell, to flattering appreciation for the women.

Under better circumstances, he probably was a hit with females.

A grim smile lingered on his lips. "Let this be a warning, all of you. If you deal with this Odell fellow, you are aiding and abetting the looting of nations deprived of their own cultural inheritance."

"Good heavens." The blonde puppy endangerer touched her throat. "You mean, like, this a con?" She tugged at her husband's sleeve.

"Of course not. Everything in this house is strictly above board." Odell sighed. "What these misguided young men mean is that they are strongly opposed to the idea of private collections, or to museums displaying any kind of artefact they have not personally authorized."

"Mock all you want." The sidekick pumped up his chest, like an angry bantam. He resembled one too, with a curl sticking up and the rest of his receding hair flopping over his ear. "Our organization is growing every day."

"Then I should advise you to return to their company and leave us alone, unless you prefer talking to the carabinieri." Odell fluttered a disdainful hand at them.

In lockstep, the two young men turned on their heels and marched out.

The offended blonde allowed herself to be escorted away, too. It was hard to tell if she'd been swayed by what I took to be protesting archaeology students from the Netherlands or one of the Nordic countries, or if she liked a grand exit.

Matt and Odell exchanged a few whispered words, and then we too were on our way.

Adriana trailed a little behind, turning her head here and there. "Back in a flash," she said as we reached the fresh air.

Without another word, she slipped back in.

Right through the closed door.

I froze. If push came to shove, she could move through walls, but never without the aid from the brick.

If the dress could give her this much strength, while separated through thick stone walls and oak doors fit for a fortress, she really had to have it, no matter what it cost.

As a last resort, I could go and beg my wealthy stepdad for money. He was generous, and nice.

The only snag was coming up with a good reason.

If I told him and my mother that I needed a cash injection to help the resident family ghost, they'd open the wallet without so much as a second thought.

The only thing is, they'd spend the money on having me whisked away for psychiatric treatment.

"Let's scram."

I jumped as Adriana almost gave me a heart attack.

Matt frowned.

Again, I pretended to wave away an insect. By now any sane man would make three crosses when he was rid of me and my weird behavior.

It shouldn't be too hard then to part with his company. Except, somehow it was.

Matt took my luggage from his car. We lingered outside the Albergo in Montepulciano that would be our home for the rest of our vacation.

"Thank you for your help," I said to Matt while Adriana amused herself with jumping, or rather floating, up onto a hotel balcony where a bird chirped away at its heart's content.

I relaxed. For once Matt should have my undivided attention.

"You've got everything?" he asked. "Or if you have any questions, give me a call. Otherwise I'll see you in three days, for the auction."

He wrote down his contact details for a hotel in Florence where he was headed in the meantime.

Adriana called down to me. "Don't stand there like a pillock. Go on, stumble and fall into his arms."

Inwardly, I gritted my teeth. Outwardly, I plastered on a big smile. "You've done so much already."

"Genie, what did I say?" my great-great-aunt admonished me.

"How about dinner's on me after the auction?" I suggested to Matt. That should satisfy her.

"It's a deal." He hefted my suitcase. "I'll just give you a hand and then I'm off."

"That's better." Adriana floated down.

She gave Matt one last wistful glance as I registered at the reception.

Her behavior gave me a pang. Was she trying to play Cupid because she had missed out on love while she was alive? Or did she attempt to keep Matt close to hang on to her own version of a love affair?

I pondered these possibilities while I followed the porter with my luggage.

Our hotel room and its balcony overlooked a park on top of the hill, which in turn overlooked medieval walls and, on the other side, smaller towns built on every hillside, all the way down to Umbria and the lakes.

Adriana drank in the view.

It was good to see my relative so content. It eased my conscience that I planned to abandon her once in a while, to have some pace and quiet.

Other than that, I would make sure that she had a ball in Italy.

As much as I believed in the power of our close bond and whatever else made her stay, I had no idea how long it would last, especially if there was no real need for her to protect me from any kind of harm.

When she first came into my life, I had supposed she needed my help to pass over for good. I still believed that she had come back for a reason, and that that reason was tied to her missing necklace and her death.

But she'd also become like a guardian angel for me. She'd saved my life when I underestimated a murderer. Also, despite a few drawbacks, I enjoyed her company.

We stayed on the balcony until the sun went down.

It didn't take much to get ready after breakfast.

Adriana clutched her newly re-acquired vanity case. I moved the brick from my purse to a small backpack. There had to be a way to lug around the darned thing without hurting myself over the next three days, until I could finally raise the auction paddle and outbid whoever else wanted the little black dress.

"We need to come up with a strategy, like Matt said," I told Adriana on our stroll through the narrow streets in the ancient town centre.

I admired the shop windows. Dressmakers, milliners, leather wares, wine sellers, and restaurants vied for my attention.

The only thing not in sight were chain stores, which made a pleasant change.

"That's going to be duck soup," she said, ogling hand-crafted gold jewelry.

"I don't think it'll be that easy."

"Only because you don't have faith in me. I can scare off those two women easy as that." She snapped her fingers. "There's also - oooh, see that ice cream?"

I could practically feel her salivate.

I did the same. There was something about the soft, scented air of an Italian day in spring, and the faint aroma from a gelateria.

I congratulated myself on only having one bread roll for breakfast, so I had space for a scoop or two.

"I want two flavors, no, three," she said. "Or better, make it four. Surprise me."

She covered her eyes as I got in line for our order.

It took the young family in front of me long enough to finish their selection to allow me to study the flavors on offer and to read a tacked-up poster about a gelato making class that began in a few days.

Other flyers offered piano lessons, English classes and jobs as a cleaner at Uni Credit and as a night guard in the Palazzo Vecchio.

Adriana kept her eyes closed as I held out the small spoon with ice cream. She sniffed. "Raspberry, with a dash of lavender." She tasted it.

It took an experienced observer like me to notice that a tiny amount of gelato had disappeared from the spoon. This was as close to properly eating as she could come. Otherwise she relied on her delicate nose to give her the sensation of food.

I swallowed the rest of the ice cream on the spoon. Then I had another spoonful and another, until I detected what I took to be a hint of lavender.

Adriana's nose was more sensitive than my tastebuds.

I offered her a sample of the next two flavors.

"Almond and coffee?"

Only mango tripped her up. Surprise, surprise. These little beauties had most likely not yet made their way to the East coast of the USA during the Roaring Twenties.

When we were both full of ice cream, I asked, "What were you saying about it being easy to secure you your Chanel dress?"

She put her hand on her hips and disappeared, into a closed shop.

I barely had rearranged my dropped jaw when she poked her head through the door, followed by the rest of her.

"Like I said, easy. If someone else coughs up more money than we have, we'll steal it."

Chapter Six

I sank onto the nearest bench. "You've got to be kid-ding me."

"It would only be taking back what is rightfully mine," Adriana pointed out.

"I'd love to see how that goes down with the officers of the law. It wasn't burglary, Your Honor, because the dress belongs to my great-great-aunt, and she needed it back."

"You won't end up in jail." She snuggled close to me. "I won't let that happen, and anyway it's me who'll do most of the work."

"I will neither end up in prison, nor in the loony bin which is where I might be heading if I listen to you. And you know why? Because I'm following the law, at home and abroad." I thumped the bench to show her I'd spoken the last word on the subject.

I might have a soft spot for my adventurous little ghost, but let the record show that Geneviève Darling can not be twisted around a spectral little finger.

Adriana took it better than I had expected, with only a slight tremble of the lips and a heartfelt sigh which might have affected me more had I not recognized these same things from the old movies I'd introduced her to.

She sighed again.

To make up for my strict rejection of embarking on a criminal career, I decided I'd show her the sights, Italian-style.

"This is amazing." Adriana held on tight as we zipped on a jade green Vespa past crumbling cream and terracotta hued houses in different stages of restoration, across meandering roads.

With the brick safe in the compartment under the seat and the warm wind in my hair, I decided to put all niggling worries aside.

This was the life I was born to live.

"Isn't it swell?" Adriana sprawled on the green grass as we paused to admire the views. Above us, cotton-candy clouds drifted across an azure sky.

I took out my sketch book. I might not be able to take photographs of my relative, but pencil drawings would do just as well.

I outlined her lying on the ground with her arms spread wide and then atop the Vespa, with an old stone wall and hills in the background.

If I used a soft wash of watercolors after our return, the sketches could go on the walls of our living room. I hoped they would fit whatever lay in store for us back home.

We weren't just in Italy on a treasure hunt and a vacation. We, or rather I, were also under strict orders to stay away while my mother and her husband had a few improvements done to the Darling villa.

That decision couldn't have come at a better time.

The owner of the work studio I'd shared for the last couple of years with my closest friend Jilly Pepper, a potter, had recently ended our lease. When Adriana came into my life, I needed to figure out what to do.

In my case, this meant taking up my mother on her offer of relocating my studio from the outskirts of New York into the garage and moving into the house for good.

Instead of a convenience apartment barely big enough to swing a cat in, I now had an entire floor to myself. Jilly would be welcome to a room too, and we could go on sharing a workspace for *Darling Designs* and *Pepper's Pots*.

It all sounded promising, if I figured out a way to make both Jilly and Adriana feel included without outing the special relationship between me and the family ghost.

My great-great-aunt was the first major secret I'd kept from my mother and my best friend. It was also the first time I'd shared a secret with a cat.

But that would have to wait. For now, I intended to enjoy every second.

As the sun set in a fiery ball, we circled back to Montepulciano, past the auction house.

"We could take a quick gander," Adriana suggested.

"No," I said. "You only get funny ideas about liberating your dress."

"I won't. I just want to feel that buzz again, for a minute or two."

The auction house lay in darkness. Street lamps were the only illumination we had.

I discreetly gazed around. I thought I spotted the uniformed guard closing the gates.

A woman waved to him from the window of a battered Fiat.

He blew her a kiss but backed away when another man, whose features had a sinister look in the dim light of the street lantern, shook his fist at him.

Something about the whole set-up struck me as odd.

It felt as if I'd spied on someone else's most private moments, when in reality all I had done was drive past, slowly. I put my foot down and we left the auction house behind.

I should have known that Adriana wouldn't give up. For someone who took an all-encompassing approach to every experience she could find, she could also demonstrate a one-track mind.

"We could visit the place for real tomorrow," she said the second we'd reached our room.

"Why?" I asked.

"Why not? The dress makes me feel all tingly and super, and I want to touch it. That's all."

"You promise?"

"Cross my heart and hope to - whatever. I trust you. And it really hurts me that you don't trust me."

I wavered. It wouldn't hurt to pay that visit, and it would make Adriana happy.

I dialed Matt's number, hoping he wouldn't wonder about receiving a call from me after ten in the evening.

"Hey there." He sounded genuinely pleased to hear from me.

A warm sensation washed over me. That must be what my great-great-aunt felt when she saw her dress. I said, "Hey. I was wondering if you could arrange another viewing for me? So I can figure out how much I'd be willing to spend on the things for my mother and for the museum? There was no direct contact on the website."

"I can try."

"Awesome."

"Tell him, as soon as possible," Adriana beseeched me.

I gave her a brief salute. "Tomorrow would be great for me," I told Matt.

"Okay, let me get back to you." A faint voice in the background called his name. A woman.

My stomach lurched for no reason at all. I hoped that Adriana hadn't heard. She would be crushed to discover that he had a private life that we didn't know about.

To keep us busy until he called back, I let my great-great-aunt give me a dance lesson in the fastest foxtrot this side of Broadway.

Which is why I greeted Matt with an "Ouch" when he got back to me.

I'd slipped on the floor and landed right on my bottom as I switched off the music while simultaneously reaching for my phone.

"Are you alright?" He seemed concerned.

"I'm fine, just bumped into something."

"Right. Here's the thing. Tomorrow's out of the question. Tristan Odell finally had the good sense to listen to me and have an approved appraiser confirm the value of the objects."

"I thought that's done automatically," I said, although in all honesty, I had no clue. My jewelry designs never broke into the lofty spheres that would be worth taking out a separate policy.

"It depends on the insurance, and the items. But what we could do is for you to have another peek in the morning of the auction," he said.

"Yes," Adriana shouted and did a Charleston twist and glide across the room.

"That's great, thanks," I said. "I'll be there at nine."

"Make it ten. I'll meet you there." He ended the call.

Adriana whirled round and round the room.

"I told you, it's going to be swell. I have the best feeling." Adriana twinkled at me.

I beamed back at her, with a naïveté I would remember forever.

As it turned out, being a ghost did not include any insights into the future, and Adriana made a useless prophet.

Chapter Seven

The morning dawned the same way pretty much every morning had dawned since Adriana had appeared - with her grinning at me the moment I opened my eyes.

"Good morning, sunshine," she sang out.

I propped myself up on my elbows.

"Look." Adriana pointed to the floor.

"What is it?" I needed caffeine to be fully awake.

Again, she pointed downwards.

I looked.

Her foot pushed my slippers half an inch, in the right position for me to slip into. A small groan told me how much effort it took her.

"I could never do that before," she said. "I think it's energy left over from the dress. Do you want me to fetch your dressing gown?"

My aging kimono hung over the sofa, on the far side of the room.

"No need. I don't want you to exhaust yourself." I sat up and patted the bed next to me. "You sit her and relax and I'll fetch us something to eat."

I threw on shirt and jeans and dashed down. A few pastries and a large latte from the buffet should be enough to keep us going.

We took our time over breakfast on the balcony. A light breeze tempered the fabled Tuscan sunshine.

Adriana basked in it. So did a cat on the balcony opposite us. The two eyed each other.

"If you want to chat with the cat, while I take a quick trip to the supermarket, go ahead," I said. "Just don't invite him or her in, or the owner might panic when he jumps over the railing."

She agreed.

I ambled past shops with free tasting of Montepulciano nobile, the famous deep red wine that had been given the seal of approval by a pope or one of his assistants back in the renaissance era.

Given the happy glow on the face of a tourist who left one of the shops, I'd better avoid this street with my great-great-aunt.

Funny how she could get tipsy without a problem, but never suffered a hangover.

A familiar scent made me swoon. Right in front of me stood a small store with hand-made reed diffusers and all kinds of lotions, including the heavenly orange blossom hand and body cream I'd used in the antique store in Livorno.

On an impulse, I bought two sets. One I intended to keep for myself, and one was destined for my mother.

Back at the hotel, my phone rang while I was putting away my purchases.

"Hello," I said.

It took me a second or so to recognize Matt's voice.

Gone was the good cheer I'd become used to.

"Are you sitting down?" he asked.

"I am now." I plopped onto the chair.

Adriana gave me a worried look.

I heard Matt swallow. "There's been a fire. In the auction house."

"Oh, no. Is the auction postponed?"

"There isn't going to be one. Most objects were destroyed, and the night guard is in the emergency care unit, in a coma."

I told myself to stay calm. "How awful."

"I'm sorry you came all the way to Italy for nothing."

"It doesn't matter," I lied. After all, he had no idea how important this sale had been for me. "As long as the guard is going to be okay."

"I'm sorry to say it's not looking good, according to Tristan Odell." Noise in the background almost drowned out his voice. "See you soon? Or are you leaving?"

I shot Adriana a sidewards glance. "I'll let you know."

"What's wrong?" Adriana pressed her hand over her lips.

If only I had any idea how to break the bad news gently. But I didn't.

"We can't get your dress. Everything up for auction went up in flames."

Chapter Eight

Adriana crumpled to the ground. Her whole body flickered and shivered.

I dropped to my knees and uttered the first words that came to my mind, inspired by a gazillion scenes playing out on the screen. "Stay with me, Adriana. Please, stay with me."

I had no idea if she could hear me, or if the shock could sever whatever link she had to me and this world.

All I knew for sure was that I didn't want to lose her.

Adriana's eyes flew open. Instead of their normal intense blue, her pupils had a silvery sheen.

I hugged her. Relief flooded through me when I sensed some kind of physical resistance.

She hadn't lost her substance.

Then her gaze met mine, and a jolt went through my system as her floodgates opened.

Under normal circumstances, I'd have been fascinated by the way I could see tears stream down her cheeks and disappear before they could touch the floor or my hands that still held her. Now, the only thing I could think of was her well-being.

"I'm so sorry," I whispered.

I threaded Adriana's arms around my neck, scooped her up, and laid her on the bed. We stayed like that for hours.

I fell asleep next to her, only to wake up with a start the next morning.

Adriana still lay where I'd put her. Gone were her smile, and her vivacity.

"I should have listened to you when you want to steal the dress," I said to her. "If there's anything I could do - I'd even break into wherever you need me to go. Just say the word."

A tiny smile was all the reaction I received from her.

I stroked her hand. "We're bound to find more of your things. We only have to keep on looking."

"What if we don't?"

When Matt called again, to ask about my plans, he sounded as down as I felt.

I was just going to answer, when I heard a voice.

"Geez Louise."

I took a double take.

Had Adriana really spoken or did I only imagine that in my mind?

Her finger pointed at the door.

I gave her a shrug. I had not idea what she meant to tell me.

"I'm still going to be here for a bit," I said into the phone, while I watched my precious ghost.

"Would you like to meet up for a coffee?" Matt asked.

I was torn.

I really, really wanted to escape for a while.

On the other hand, what if anything happened to my great-great-aunt while I was gone?

She lifted her head and pointed at the door again. Her eyes were back to blue, but not as intensively azure as they should be. "Go," she whispered. "I'll get over the shock by myself."

"Okay," I said as much to her as to Matt.

Adriana sank back onto the bed as I glanced back.

I'd never seen her so despondent.

A little later, when I sat with Matt at a table outside a café in the piazza, I did my best to ignore my fear for Adriana and put on a brave face.

So did Matt.

I'd only known him for a couple of months, but he'd always been resourceful, almost unflappable.

Now, his eyes were heavy-lidded and his left hand clenched and unclenched.

"Tell me," I said. "Is it about the fire?"

"Paolo, the security guard, died this morning from smoke inhalation, without regaining consciousness." His shoulders hunched. "The firefighters had to break into his room at the auction house. The door was locked, from the outside."

The breath caught in my chest. "But surely that's impossible. Unless --"

"Yes. The police believe that someone locked the room on purpose. It was also where the fire extinguishers were kept."

"How horrible. But the sprinklers -- "

I thought back to the Palazzo Vecchio. I remembered a glimpse of something red in the small side room. That must have been the extinguishers.

What I did not recall were any sprinklers in the ornately painted ceiling.

"There weren't any," Matt confirmed. "The installation would have been impossible without damaging the artwork. The security cameras were off as well. The police think they're dealing with arson and murder, and Tristan Odell is their main suspect."

My head whirled. "Why would he do that?"

"Insurance fraud. It's not uncommon."

"But why now? And he of all people would have been aware of the guard being there. I can't believe he'd deliberately lock the man in and let him die. That's monstrous."

"That's exactly what I thought at first, but what if he had no idea Paolo slept in the room? The guard had just recently asked for a daytime job. That's why he was wearing the uniform when you met him. He wanted to work more sociable hours, to have a normal private life."

"You seem to have a lot of information." Matt must have excellent contacts, I thought. Or be close to someone the police would open up to.

His jaw tightened. "I'm the one who pressured Odell into officially consulting an insurance appraiser. That's what made the police and the insurance company suspicious in the first place. With all the merchandise in the main room destroyed, there is no way to decide if their value was overstated or not."

"But how would that profit Odell?" I sipped my now lukewarm cappuccino. "I thought he was only the auctioneer."

"For most of the items in the catalog, yes. But a dozen things also came from his private collection, and then there's the insurance money for the building. It appears he wasn't exactly swimming in money."

"I'm sorry," I said. "But don't blame yourself. Even if you were the catalyst, you couldn't have had any inkling of what was going to happen."

"That's what I tell myself. Or at least I try to." He made a wry grimace. "I have no idea why I burden you with this, except that you're a good listener, and you're smart. If Odell is innocent, I don't think he's got any chance to prove it, without help."

"I'm not a detective," I protested.

"You did solve a murder case before."

"Only because I was on the spot, and I had a lot more access to information." Not to mention I had the invaluable help of my very own pet whisperer, which made it easier to find trustworthy witnesses on four legs.

I fidgeted. I'd been gone for longer than planned already.

"I'll be around for a couple of days." Matt put down the money for our coffees. "If you change your mind or have any idea, I'd really appreciate your help, Genie."

I gave him a noncommittal nod. "I'll think about it."

I found Adriana as I left her, huddled under the blanket and devastated.

"How are you feeling?" I hurried to pile up everything of Adriana's around her, to re-energize her as much as possible.

When I touched the brick, my finger caught on a rough end from the breakage. I thought I'd glued the broken piece on so it fit exactly, but apparently I was mistaken.

She flinched a little as I scraped my nail over the excess glue.

"Is that what's making you weak?" I asked. "Did you feel the dress burn?" The very thought made me feel sick.

Inch by inch, she lifted herself up on her elbow.

A faint tinge of pink came into her cheeks.

The color of her pupils deepened as she pondered this. "I didn't feel anything. Not a twinge, not a nip, not a tingle. Do you understand what that means?"

"Of course I do." I beamed so hard at her my face came close to splitting in two. "You'll be fine once you've overcome the bombshell."

"Not just that, Genie. It means my little black dress still exists, and we can go and pinch it." She jumped into my arms so enthusiastically that I felt myself move an inch or two. Adriana was back.

She wiggled her fingers. "So, where do we start? Picking locks for practice?"

CHAPTER NINE

I had no idea if I was more excited or more scared to have Adriana full of vigour again.

"You did promise you'd break into wherever we have to." She slid over the floor with the best dance style I'd seen this side of Ginger Roger.

That decided it for me.

Scared was the correct option.

"That was before Matt told me the guard has been murdered," I cautioned.

Adriana's eyes widened. "Are you sure?"

"Pretty much. There's a lot I would do to put my hands on your dress, but I'm not sure at this stage there's anything we can do." Anything, expect figuring why the dress wasn't gone after all, who had it now in their possession, and if its prolonged existence had something to do with the death of the guard and the fire that caused said demise.

Poor Paolo. I'd only seen him once in action and once from afar, but I could envisage him in my mind, down to the tattoo on his hand.

"You don't mean it that we should sit around and do nothing," she protested. "We can't allow a murderer and dress-thief to get away with it."

"If those two things are connected," I said.

"In that case, all we would do is search for my dress." She gave me a pleading look that tugged at my heart-strings. "It means everything to me. I told you Belle gave it to me."

"But we are going to keep out of the police's way."

She crossed her heart. "Absolutely."

In this case, we needed a game plan, and we needed it fast.

Since I had no idea how far Adriana's personal radar went, the longer it took us to solve the mystery, the greater became the risk that the dress would be out of our reach.

A tiny voice at the back of my mind reminded me that there was also a murderer on the loose. I pushed that thought aside. We would steer clear of any dangerous move. If in doubt, I could leave things to Matt, consider-ing he'd tried to enlist me as a sleuthing partner.

"What do we know, and where do we start?" I pulled out my notebook and pen and wrote the question down.

"The staff," Adriana said. "There must be a cleaner or caretaker or whoever does the work." She frowned. "I wish they had a guard dog, not just that poor man."

"True, but then maybe the dog would have died too." We shared a horrified moment.

"There might be other dogs in the neighborhood. We could ask them," Adriana pointed out.

"We could, if you're sure you're up to another trip on the Vespa?."

She crossed her arms and gave me a withering look.

I'd expected a tarred ruin. Instead, only the soot on the outer walls and an acrid smell in the air gave away what had happened two nights ago in the Palazzo Vecchio.

The idea of police tape didn't bother me, and not just because I didn't spot any.

We'd only come to search for witnesses of the animal persuasion. The last thing I intended to do was to go inside a burnt-out place that had led to the death of a man.

I led Adriana away from the gate to the auction house. About fifty yards away, I spotted a familiar looking battered Fiat parked outside a coffee bar.

Inside, a middle-aged woman sobbed at the shoulder of a waitress. As she lifted her head to wipe away her tears, it confirmed my idea.

This was the same woman I'd seen flirting with Paolo.

And she had a small terrier by her side.

"Can you interview the dog while I try my luck with the women?" I asked Adriana.

She gave me an enthusiastic nod.

I pushed the door open, crossing my fingers that my smattering of Italian would garner me some goodwill, and that the grieving woman or the waitress spoke enough English to be of use.

"Buongiorno," I said.

Under a glass counter stood plates with fresh pastries.

I ordered a cappuccino and an almond croissant. Then I settled at the bar and waited for an opening.

Adriana crouched next to the little terrier. His ears twitched as she spoke to him in hushed whispers.

The woman next to me stopped crying. Dark circles ringed her mournful eyes. The handkerchief she used to wipe them was almost as tear-soaked as her face.

"Are you okay?" My tone hopefully hit the right mix of friendly concern and sisterly understanding. The waitress gave me a little shrug.

I added, "What happened to the auction house across the street? I heard someone mention a fire."

Paolo's sweetheart broke into a new flood of tears. "He's gone, my fiancé is gone and nothing can bring him back." She buried her head in her hands. A lump formed inside my stomach.

The waitress signaled to somebody outside the bar.

The next thing I knew, the crying woman flung herself in the arms of a burly man with grazed knuckles, a cigarette behind his ear, and the word Mamma tattooed between two hearts on his bare arm.

I'd also seen him before.

He was the guy who'd shaken his fist at Paolo.

The dog woofed a little. He gazed adoringly at my great-great-aunt as his owner swooped him up. She leant on the newcomer for support as they left.

"Have a chinwag with the waitress," Adriana said.

"I'm sorry if I upset your customer," I said, following my orders. The croissant crumbled between my fingers.

"It's not your fault." The waitress clucked her tongue. "Such a tragedy."

"What happened? An accident?"

"Maybe yes, maybe no. The carabinieri don't say, but there's been a lot of people going in and out of the palazzo."

She took away my empty cup.

Adriana frowned. She loved the milk foam, especially with a few chocolate sprinkles on top, even if one or two drops were all she could manage.

"Another cappuccino, please," I said.

The coffee machine whirred.

I could see myself mirrored in its polished metal.

Next to me, I spotted Adriana lick her lips in anticipation. Everybody else would only notice an empty stool beside me.

I wondered if the terrier had really seen her or just felt her presence and heard her voice.

I also wondered what he had told her.

"And the signora's fiancé died? How horrible. When my aunt lost her boyfriend, we were so glad she had a friend who took care of her. They married a year later." I attempted a wan smile.

"Chiara has nobody." The waitress made a tragic face. "To think they'd only found each other again, and then, pouf, all happiness gone."

I held a spoon with milk foam up, so Adriana could dip her finger in it. "Oh. I thought ..." Most people could not resist filling in the blanks, if they were offered the chance.

The waitress was no exception. "You mean, Luigi? He's Chiara's brother, so he doesn't count when it comes to her broken heart."

Interesting, I mused. Luigi definitely had disliked the victim, and those grazes on his knuckles had been fresh.

Maybe they stemmed from breaking into a building or from knocking out a man before locking him in?

I had no way to know if the latter assumption was correct, but I wanted to believe that Paolo had already been unconscious before the fire broke out.

The alternative was too awful to contemplate.

"He seemed nice," I said, hoping she'd tell me more.

She shrugged. "It's family." With that, a group of Dutch tourists entered, and the conversation was over.

"I think we're on the right track," I told Adriana as we climbed onto the Vespa.

"Are we ever. You'll never guess what I found out." She clung to my waist. "We're the best detectives in the world."

We weaved along the narrow roads.

To my eternal gratitude, in front of us drove one of the ubiquitous little three-wheeled vans that had a small cabin in front and an open trailer at the back. Not only did their period appeal add to the scenery, although some of Piaggio's Ape50 appeared to be new, they also allowed me to ride at a sedate pace without being honked at every single minute by the sportier drivers.

In the land of Ferrari and Maserati, the need for speed was alive and thriving, whereas I preferred to stay alive by taking it slow.

Adriana flitted towards our room but had the grace to wait until I unlocked the door instead of oozing through.

There was something about watching her going through walls that gave me the willies, if I was unprepared.

I gulped down a glass of water. "I'm listening."

"Gigi," she said. "That's his name. And he told me that Chiara's brother and Paolo had it in for each other. Chiara and Paolo used to be sweethearts in high school, but then he left her for another girl, and it took him 30 years to meet her again and win her back. Romantic, isn't it?"

A longing expression flitted over her face. Considering she'd breathed her last when she was only 21 years old, she'd missed out on a lot of things, including a reunion with a long lost lover.

It also saved her a lot of wear and tear on her heart.

I said, "I've got to admit, I'm with the brother. If Paolo dumped Chiara in his youth for another girl, odds are he'd have done the same again, one day. Not that I'm condoning violence or anything."

I tried not to sound bitter, but I was speaking from experience. Taking back an old flame rarely went well.

"That's what brother Luigi told her, and then he huffed off, into the night. When he came back, there was blood on his knuckles, and Gigi reckons Luigi played some serious chin music, loud and clear." She feigned a few uppercuts.

My pulse increased.

Could the solution be that simple? Were we dealing with a fight that had gone out of hand, and a fire to cover up the real crime?

"Did Gigi tell you when that was?" I asked.

If Luigi had come back bloodied the night of the arson, that clinched it.

It would also explain the utter desolation of Chiara.

Losing a fiancé was bad enough.

Having your own brother be the one responsible for losing him, took it to a whole new level, if she knew or only suspected.

Adriana shook her head, no. "Gigi said they never saw Paolo again, and he would know, because he was always hanging out with Chiara, when he had the chance. Gigi swears that Paolo was the nicest man Chiara had ever gone out with." The corners of her mouth turned down.

"Has she told the police anything?" Maybe they had already shifted their target from Tristan Odell to brother Luigi.

Adrianna shrugged, still sad. "Gigi couldn't say."

A physical fight left visible signs. The doctors and nurses were bound to have noticed them when Paolo was admitted.

Matt would know, and if he didn't, he'd be glad to hear there was another suspect.

I just had to gloss over my source a little.

CHAPTER TEN

Matt answered my call after two ring tones.

Like usual, he appeared pleased to hear from me, and he sounded happier still when I told him that I would indeed be willing to support his investigation.

"Word on the street is, Paolo had a future brother-in-law who wasn't exactly a fan," I said. "There's talk about a fight between them, on the night in question."

He whistled through his teeth. "Interesting. I had no idea, and neither did Tristan Odell. How did you discover that so fast?"

Modesty and subterfuge in equal parts compelled me to say, "I was lucky. I stumbled upon the grieving fiancée, and her friend happened to open up to a few sympathetic words."

"And a sympathetic face."

"That, too." I caught myself preening a little. "Any news on your end? Where is Odell?"

In my mind I saw ancient prisons, with their mile thick walls, foul straw and tiny barred apertures.

I shuddered. Places like the Bridge of Sighs in Venice were fun to visit, but not so much joy if you were the one on the inside.

The same went for any other prison, really. We'd walked past a torture museum in Montepulciano. That was one museum you couldn't pay me to visit.

"He was told to make himself available and not to go away. He did receive permission to move into a hotel in Arezzo. I can understand why he didn't want to stay in his rooms at the back end of the complex while everything is up in the air."

"Was he the one who discovered the fire?" To be honest, I had no clue why I asked that or what the answer could tell me. The first case Adriana and I had solved had relied as much on luck as on clever deduction on our side.

"A neighbor raised the alarm. Odell was out with friends in Florence, an hour away," he said.

"Doesn't that give him an alibi?"

"Unless the friends, a poker group of Brits and Americans living in Italy half the year, were covering for him, or he set an accelerant, or he hired another person to do the job for him."

"All good points." Something else niggled. "You're really worried, aren't you? It feels like it's deeply personal to you, apart from the affair maybe being related to that appraisal you set in motion."

"Is it that obvious?" Matt asked.

Adriana shouted into the phone, "Hello, Genie and I are sleuths, we can smell a rat a mile away."

"He can't hear you," I mouthed.

Into the phone, I said, "For an observant listener like me, you mean?"

"Tristan Odell used to be at university with my boss."

"You don't want to break the news to your superior that his old friend could go down for a long spell in prison and have killed an innocent man."

"Her old friend, and no, I really don't want to do that. Also, I like the guy."

We both fell silent.

"Do you have a way to let it be known that the fiancée's brother is at least as likely?" I asked.

"I'll figure it out."

Just as I was about to end the conversation, Adriana tugged at her dress. "My Chanel, ask him about my little black Chanel dress."

"Just one more question, out of curiosity," I told Matt. "How can you or the insurance be sure that all the items really were destroyed in the fire? What if for example somebody helped himself to a couple of things and sold them? Security wasn't that great, after all."

The silence lasted so long that I wondered if something had happened to Matt.

"You mean Odell?" he asked.

"Not specifically. Anyone with access to the auction rooms and a way to sell a few choice antiques would do. It's not like you could put them on a flea market stall, but some of the stuff would probably fetch a decent price if you knew a buyer."

I eyeballed the catalog. Even at the lower end of the estimated auction price, a small number of select thefts would bring in a nice bundle of money.

"The owner would be the first choice," Matt mused.

"Can you check out the finances of our guys? Odell, Luigi, and Paolo?"

"The dead guard? Why?"

"Simply because he's the victim does not necessarily exclude his involvement in anything shady. What if he sold stolen goods to the wrong person or disappointed the wrong guys?"

"The mob." Adriana clapped her hands. "Al Capone and Lucky Luciano were Italian. I had no idea thugs like those two are still around."

I covered the microphone, so Matt would be unable to hear me. "Big time," I assured her.

"That's a thought," Matt admitted. "I'll see if I can pull some strings."

"One more thing," I added after a few whispered words from my sidekick. "Do we have a timeline for the events?"

I made notes of everything he said however little it was, and we promised to keep each other updated.

Because I'm basically an honest woman, I kept my fingers crossed behind my back while we were speaking.

Even if I wanted to tell him the truth, the whole truth, and nothing but the truth, it wasn't going to happen.

Swallowing the notion of a stunning young ghost would be hard enough, but relying on the testimony of dogs might be a step too far for anyone not currently in the room with me.

Operation Chanel needed to be kept on the down-low from Matt.

"What do we do now?" Adriana asked.

"Search for a few more witnesses."

Chapter Eleven

One look at the streets, where the drivers appeared to be infected with racing fever as they ignored the narrow streets and sharp corners, made me blanche. For once I ignored the Vespa and had the receptionist call me a taxi.

The chauffeur sang along to "Volare" and other classics beloved by my late grandmother, and now, my great-great-aunt as well. Since Adriana made up her own lyrics, I broke into a giggle which I masked with a tissue when the driver shot me a hurt glance in the front mirror.

At least he almost kept to the speed limit.

We arrived at the scene of the crime in the final hour of the lunch break. This meant less humans, because the few smaller shops were closed.

The bar and the pet store were the only exceptions.

A few dogs sat inside the shops or peered from balconies.

Only a golden retriever rested on his haunches outside the bar.

Cats seemed to be everywhere, basking in the sun. I spotted two on doorsteps, on the saddle of a motorbike, and one grooming herself while perched on a chair in a doorway.

We made a beeline for the retriever.

He turned his head as Adriana stopped a foot away and gazed at her with the milky eyes of an old, half blind animal.

His muzzle had faded to white.

As likable as he was, I had little expectation that he could be useful. I stayed back while she approached him.

Most old dogs were at least half deaf, and I had no intention on startling him.

"Get a move on," Adriana told me. "Meet my new friend, Ettore."

I followed Adriana's instructions, including how to ruffle Ettore's ears.

Gratefully, he sniffed my hands.

I ruffled his ears some more.

He rubbed his head against my legs, leaving hairs on my jeans.

Adriana and he started a conversation until I interfered. "What is he saying?"

"That he woke up from the stink in the air, and then the noise from engines and men shouting and water whooshing."

"Did he notice anything else, before that?"

Ettore's ears twitched as she spoke to him in guttural noises that he seemed to understand just fine.

I wished that only once I'd be able to listen in to their chat.

Adriana shook her head. "Only that Luigi and Paolo had a fight, earlier in the evening."

"A fist fight?"

"He says no, only with words, but he did not like the voices. They made the ruff on his neck stand up. They calmed down just as he was thinking he should go and help Paolo."

"Why would he want to do that?"

She made a few guttural sounds, and he responded in low woofs.

"Because Paolo and he used to work together. Ettore says the two of them were like this when he was younger." Adriana pressed two fingers together to demonstrate the closeness.

"He used to be a guard dog? Matt never mentioned a dog." A cold fear gripped me. "Did the killer also kill an animal?"

The idea brought back the full horror of Paolo's death.

Ettore gave me a quick, reassuring lick with his rough tongue.

I rummaged in my purse for my newly purchased hand cream. As pleasant as the dog was, his breath did not smell like roses, or orange blossoms. I wiped my hands clean and lavishly treated them.

"No," Adriana confirmed. "When the owner decided that Ettore should be given the bum rush, Paolo arranged for him to be adopted by the bar manager. There was no replacement because the lady of the house had a thing about having animals around and put her foot down. Paolo couldn't keep Ettore in his small apartment."

Adriana's grimace mirrored mine. Being animal lovers was another thing that had been passed down the Darling line.

"I thought Odell was a bachelor," I said, trying to envisage him. No, he definitely hadn't worn a wedding band. "And kicking out your own dog is mean and cruel." The idea made me lose all sympathy for the man. I wondered if Matt had heard about Ettore.

"He didn't own the joint back then," Adriana said. "It belonged to another couple."

"So, Paolo came with the place," I mused.

"He did, and he came to visit Ettore all the time and bring him a nice juicy bone."

Ettore hung his head.

"I'm sorry, buddy." I stroked him.

He sucked in the air and growled.

Had I upset him?

"If that doesn't take the dog biscuit," Adriana marveled. "Ettore's one heck of a witness, let me tell you that." She made a dramatic pause.

"What did he say?"

"He only gave us the best clue yet." She did a shimmy.

"You mean, our first clue, apart from the deduction that the dress somehow is still around?"

"Ettore says, when he went for his final stroll that night, there was someone sneaking up on to the property. He didn't think much of it then, but it must have been right before the whole affair went down."

"He saw someone?"

Ettore blinked, and my hopes evaporated.

The dog had his heart in the right place, but I'd be surprised if he could spot anything further away than his food bowl.

"He heard steps." Another dramatic pause, intended to keep me on tenterhooks.

It worked. "Did he recognize them?"

"He's a golden retriever, not a miracle worker. But he told me something at least as good." She did a quick twirl. "The thug smelt like you."

I was confused.

"Your fingers. Whoever it was, he carried a whiff of your hand cream."

"Are you sure Ettore said, he?" Now I did a dance step.

There shouldn't be too many men around who preferred floral scents for their cosmetics.

"I think so. He can't really tell with only using his nose, can he? But he caught another smell, a stronger one, a little like tobacco, without the burn."

Sadly, that told me nothing, especially since a huge number to Italians still smoked and even walked around in shops with an unlit cigarette in their hand, ready to light up at the first instance.

Ettore drooped. The old boy needed his sleep.

"Thank you," I told him.

"What now?" Adriana patted his flank.

We both glanced around and saw the grey cat on the chair arch her back in a luxurious stretch.

Adriana high-fived me.

Chapter Twelve

Adriana ambled up to the large grey cat.

I decided to hang back a little, until we could be sure the feline didn't mind being questioned.

I had a handful of treats in my pocket, in case we needed to resort to a little bribery.

Adriana motioned me to freeze. I did, until the cat wiped her ears with her paw, which I took as a peace signal.

I moved closer, until I could touch my great-great-aunt. She made a few humming sounds at the back of her throat.

The cat answered with a high pitched meow. Adriana nodded.

I trod from one foot to another.

The first shop door had just opened, and customers were heading our way.

I didn't want them to spook the grey cat, or for Chiara and her brother to come along and wonder what we were doing here, again.

In a big city, running into the same strangers was a lot easier to ignore than in a small town, outside of the main attractions.

Sweat formed on my forehead.

I blamed the relentless sunshine that blazed from the sky.

The grey cat meowed again and swished her tail before she settled back for a nap. The interview was over.

We moved on to the next cat, a few steps away, who hissed at the grey feline and swiped her paw at her with unsheathed claws.

Adriana chuckled.

"What's so funny?" I asked.

"His comment is." My still chortling great-great-aunt motioned to a multi-colored tom cat with a piratical expression on his face, thanks to a black patch over his left eye. "He said that old queen is the sour puss of the hood."

"Does Pirate Cat have anything else to say?" I'd have given a lot to be able to hear for myself, or ask pertinent questions. As hard as I tried, I wasn't too good at this whole relying on everyone else thing.

Adriana clasped my hand.

I could barely tell where my fingers ended and hers began, just like I couldn't tell where the raspy voice in my head really came from.

All I knew for certain was, that I heard words.

"Now, capisce, I only do this for Paolo," the voice said. "He was a good man, always ready with a bit of fish or chicken or a shady spot. He rescued one of my kittens once from a tree. Not that the little one needed rescuing, not if it was much like me, the greatest climber in all of these hills, the strongest runner, the toughest fighter ..."

My knees grew weak. I could understand him, as well as Adriana.

She practically purred at the cat. "I bet there's nothing going on here without you having the goods."

"It's my job, as capo of this quartiere." Pirate Cat hissed and swiped at imaginary things.

I chuckled to myself. Flattery worked as well on male cats as it did on two-legged males.

Adriana continued. "I also bet you noticed the fire straight away, and anything going on right before."

He studied the ground under his feet. "There's an ant. See that ant?"

Adriana's voice softened. "So it's true what we heard? You had no idea?"

The tom cat glowered at her. "I was on patrol, that's what happened, capisce? I was following those couple of rock throwing two-legged morons. A capo has many responsibilities."

"You chased someone?" Adriana asked.

"All the way up to Nonna's. Nobody else could have done that."

He lost us there. Nonna meant Grandma, which in this case meant nothing to me.

"What do you think? Is that information worth something?" He sniffed the air, in the direction of my pocket with the cat treats.

I put down a handful for him.

Adriana staggered. She let go of me. "I don't feel that hot," she said. "I'm all woozy."

Pirate Cat tucked into his goodies. He meowed but there were no more words in my head.

"Thank you," I said to him as much as to Adriana. I steadied her. "Let's not do that mind connection thing again if it drains you that much."

Her meek acceptance worried me a little.

I'd expected her to pretend everything was peachy. She usually did.

So, when Matt sent me a message to invite me out to dinner, I decided to let my great-great-aunt rest and go out without her as my chaperone.

Back in our hotel room, I put a prepaid phone on the table and switched it on. "This has got my number stored. If anything happens at all or you feel faint, say, Alexa, call Genie. It won't be able to catch your voice but it might react to your vibrations."

Adriana whispered, "Alexa, call Genie."

My phone rang.

"It works! Now try to switch it off."

She pressed her fingertips against her temples and concentrated.

The screen went dark. The ceiling lamp followed.

"Can you switch it on again?"

Adriana's impact on electricity tended to be slightly erratic in crucial moments, which was the main reason I'd ruled out flying with her.

I had no idea if she could knock out a plane's systems, but I definitely did not plan to put it to the test.

She tried harder. Both phone and lamp sprang to life.

"Perfect," I said. "And as a last resort, try to press down here." I showed Adriana where to place her fingertips, in the hope her energy would transfer itself. That should allow her to call me to her side if she needed me to give her strength.

I left with Adriana's blessing, and dressed to her specifications in a jade silk shirt and relaxed jeans.

To her disappointment I'd declined to wear heels.

One of the drawbacks on the ancient cities of Tuscany were the worn flagstones leading up and down the narrow, badly lit alleys in the centers.

I congratulated myself on my foresight when I watched a woman clutch her partner's arm in a last ditch attempt to keep upright after slipping on the smooth surface.

The next thing I knew, I almost went down myself.

A few steps ahead of me stood two young men, engrossed in what appeared to be an urgent discussion.

I'd last seen them creating a ruckus at the auction house, and here they were again, right under a sign for "Nonna's Albergo".

They had to be Pirate Cat's rock-throwing morons.

The question was, how far would they have gone to take back the sculpture they'd gone on about from Tristan Odell - far enough to kill?

Chapter Thirteen

"Genie, meet Serina." Matt introduced me to a modern day Sophia Loren. She was in her early forties dressed in a suit which hugged her body without being overly revealing.

One glance at her, and I felt hopelessly underdressed and outclassed in every way. That is, until she greeted me with two air kisses and an original Genie Darling design touched my cheek.

This fabulous woman wore chandelier earrings reminiscent of Egyptian revival, hand-made by no other than myself.

"Serina is the appraiser I told you about," Matt said as we sat down in the back room of a restaurant that oozed rustic authenticity.

I waited for more explanation. And I decided to not be disappointed that I'd misread the situation a tiny bit.

This dinner with me was obviously strictly business. I wondered what Serina had to do with it or what my role was supposed to be.

A thought popped up in my head.

Had I been right?

Was the arson supposed to cover up brazen thefts?

Did they want me, as an eyewitness for the original viewing, to confirm the lack of evidence that should have been there?

Clothes could be destroyed completely by fire.

Gemstones and metals were different, they would pretty much always be left in some form or another.

I frowned under the cover of the menu until I reminded myself to copy Serina and relax my face.

I could make a few educated guesses if I saw what was left from precious jewelry, but not enough to be considered an absolute authority.

That should be Serina's metier.

"You should try the fish," Serina said. "It's fresh from the lakes."

Since I was chomping at the bit to figure out what on earth I was doing here, I asked her to choose for me. That sort of trust tended to put people at ease.

I'd also never had a single bad meal in Italy yet, so being agreeable came risk-free.

Matt went for steak and then was maddeningly quiet.

I decided to take the bull by the horns. "What have you found out? Or is this simply a social call?"

He and Serina exchanged an inscrutable glance.

He gave her a tiny nod.

"Matt says you were the one who came up with a couple of starting points for us to look into," she said.

"Yes?" I waited for her to go on.

"Tristan Odell has outstanding debts. We're talking easily six figures here." A tiny crease formed between her perfectly arched brows. "Debt he could pay off with the insurance money."

"Oh." I thought back to the suave Englishman, and to Paolo with his pride in his uniform and his kindness towards animals. "That would be a strong motive. What happened? Did he gamble?"

The hint of a smile lightened her features. "Italy happened. He got carried away with restoring his palazzo to its former glory. Marble from Carrara, repairing the ceilings and making sure the frescoes and murals would still be intact in another century costs money. A lot of money." Her voice became strangely flat.

"You don't believe it or you do and you'd rather you were wrong," I deduced.

"It fits the facts," she said as the waiter brought the salads to start us off.

"What exactly are the facts? How did the fire start?" I bit into the juiciest tomato I'd had in years and relished the taste. "Was it an inside job, with somebody tampering with the wiring to make it appear an accident, or was there an accelerant?"

"I haven't received the report yet." Serina pouted.

"We've also looked into the dead guard's finances," Matt said. "He'd recently taken half his savings out of his bank account."

"That doesn't look like he was stealing from Odell and selling the stuff," I said. "Unless he was being black-mailed over something and threatened to tell on who-ever it was."

"We thought of that. Until the police found a receipt in Paolo's apartment. He'd spent the money on a diamond ring for his fiancée."

That fit in with the picture the animals had given us of their old friend. I was glad I could cross him off our suspect list. Adriana would be relieved too.

I wondered how I could bring up the two suspicious protesters. "Do you have photos of the crime scene?"

She pointed at her fashionably small purse which could barely fit a phone and a lipstick. "Not on me. Why?"

"Because it would be good to see for myself if anything looks out of the ordinary, compared to when I saw it. What I don't understand is how Paolo could be trapped in the place."

"I told you, his room was locked and the key was missing," Matt said and then stopped when the waiter appeared with our food.

"Yes, but that doesn't explain why he didn't call for help. He must have had a phone. Why didn't he use it?" I wondered aloud.

"He was drunk. It appears he and his future brother-in-law had sorted out their issues over too much strong beer. Paolo wasn't a heavy drinker, by all accounts, so that could be why he didn't react."

"What about these other guys, the two protesters Paolo saw off the premises?" I asked.

Serina gave me a quizzing look. "Who are you talking about?"

So, she didn't know about them.

Interesting - probably.

Matt thought so too. "That should be in the report."

"I'll look into it," she said when my phone rang and I dropped my fork.

My heart raced as I pressed, answer, only to hear my mother's cheerful voice.

"What do you think about peacocks?"

"What?" My mother has many wonderful qualities. They could also be maddening, like her preference to drop all preliminaries when least expected.

She went on, "I've found this rather marvelous silk screen with a 1920s peacock print, and Jolene said she could find matching wallpaper for a feature wall in your apartment. I wanted to surprise you, but then we thought, better check with you first."

"Right. Let me think about it."

It was a nice touch that my mother through herself wholeheartedly into the renovation of the old Darling villa, including what was to be my private floor and my studio.

It also came at the worst time.

"Don't wait too long," Jolene's chipper voice came thorough loud enough to make Matt listen up. "Is my cousin around?" she asked.

"He's right here. Do you want me to hand you over?" I asked her.

Jolene had the distinction of being Cobblewood Cove's Girl Friday. There was nothing she couldn't do when it came to drilling, building, or fixing things around the house.

She'd also become my friend within a short span of time.

We were close in age, and she and Matt were as thick as thieves.

He already reached out his hand to take my phone when another call came in.

"Adriana" flashed across the screen.

"Sorry, bye. I've got another urgent call." I cut off Jolene and took a deep steadying breath as I hit "accept".

I could barely make out Adriana's words. "There's something outside our door."

I pushed back my chair and flashed Matt and Serina an apologetic look. "I've got to go, I'm really sorry."

I sprinted out of the restaurant. "Adriana, I'm on my way."

Chapter Fourteen

Outside, a cool breeze had sprung up, and yet I was beginning to sweat. "Hang in there," I begged her. Why, o why did I choose to walk?

The Vespa would have carried me to the albergo in less than five minutes.

I listened closely. Over the phone, I could make out a faint boom - boom - boom amid other noises.

It sounded vaguely familiar. Then it was gone.

"That was a close shave," my great-great-aunt whispered. I couldn't tell if she was frightened but I was.

"Stay on the phone until I'm back," I told her.

"Can you bring me ice-cream?"

"What? Why?"

"Chocolate, please, and cherry and almond."

With that, she was gone.

My pulse slowly went back to normal as a tap on my shoulder made me spin around.

"Everything okay?" Matt peered at me. I hadn't even heard him following me. "You look like you've seen a ghost."

If only. I gave him a rueful smile. "Sorry to run out on you two. It was from the hotel, about weird noises from my room. Probably a feline visitor or some other critter." I chuckled. "In any case, they asked me to check that everything's okay."

As far as explanations went, this sounded at least remotely plausible.

"Shall I drive you?"

"No need, but thanks for the offer. Give my regards to Serina, and we'll talk soon?"

I hurried off, glad the gelateria was on my direct route.

I asked the girl behind the counter for separate tubs and a carry bag.

Whatever my great-great-aunt wanted the dessert for, she would get it.

While my ice-cream was lovingly put in its containers, I studied the noticeboard again.

The ad for the gelato-making class was still hanging there, and so was the one advertising the job as night guard for the Palazzo Vecchio.

I could almost hear the clicks in my brain as I made the connection.

That job offer must be for Odell's auction house.

I handed over the money to pay, when I heard an American order a double scoop of vegan coffee ice-cream.

I recognized the voice.

It seemed the Stones were still in town, despite the loss of their miniatures and lack of vintage items to purchase.

Adriana lounged on the sofa, with a P. G. Wodehouse audiobook playing. She put a finger to her lips as she saw me. "That Jeeves is a hoot," she said. "You have to listen to this."

"Later," I said.

Obediently, she paused the narration.

I filled a large spoonful of each ice cream flavor on a saucer. While she sniffed at them like a rapturous puppy I gave her the once-over.

Whatever had frightened her into calling me had caused no lingering side-effects, from what I could gather.

She switched on her audiobook again, a lot louder than necessary.

I reached for the pause button when a noise from next door startled me.

Boom - boom - boom.

Adriana nearly jumped out of her skin.

I cocked my head towards the wall. The sound came from the adjoining room.

Another boom made me dash towards the door when a groggy voice cried out, "Basta, stop it with your loud talking, my baby wants to sleep."

It took me a moment before I made the connection to the audiobook. "Scusi," I called out and paused Stephen Fry as the inimitable butler Jeeves mid-sentence.

I wiped my brow. "That's one less worry. From now on, we'll be quiet, okay? You have excellent hearing anyway."

"I do." Adriana inhaled the ice-cream aroma again.

My phone pinged, again, and again.

Jolene had sent me pictures of the painted screen, and wallpaper samples, and decoration ideas that fit in with my jewelry designs.

She'd also added a text, "Hey, girlfriend, before your mom commits to major changes, have a peek. If you want to go with a period theme, I can also get my hands on a few sconces and a chandelier and so on, but the brackets and fixings would be more modern. And tell my cousin to bring me back some seriously chic swag from his vacay."

Adriana brightened up. "Let me have a gander. I'm going to live in those rooms too."

We scrolled through the pictures together, and she made me jot down a few ideas of her own.

"You should make sketches and send them," she suggested.

"That's not a bad idea. Except, I'd have to visualize what the rooms look like right now."

She gave me an exasperated eye-roll. "If you can't remember, Jolene can do a tour and deliver everything you need. Although you're a bit young to have a bad memory."

I grimaced. "Can you do better?"

She shrugged as she rattled off more details about the Darling villa than I thought possible, and not only things that would have stuck after growing up in the place.

She could describe everything including the things I'd brought, down to the number of books.

I felt my excitement grow.

If Adriana had a near photographic memory, crime scene pictures might reveal new clues to her.

Despite the evidence against him, I had a hard time picturing Tristan Odell setting fire to a place he loved so much he'd piled up huge debts to restore it, or that he would be so ruthless to sacrifice Paolo's life.

What I could imagine was two young men deciding that throwing rocks in protest wasn't enough.

What if they'd returned, fueled by self-righteousness and whatever they drank or smoked, and had broken in to steal objects they decided should not be there, before starting a fire?

Adriana pondered this suggestion when I put it to her.

"What about Paolo?" she asked.

"That's the bit I only realized tonight. Can you recollect the small side room?"

"Sure."

"What exactly did you see?"

"A bucket. A sand bag. Two fire extinguishers. Parts of a cabinet."

"Exactly." I grinned. "No bed in sight. It would have been easy to overlook that the room could also be used for sleeping. Especially if you'd seen this flyer."

I showed her the picture I'd taken. "Translated, it says, Night guard wanted, for immediate start. Apply directly at the Palazzo Vecchio auction house. They must have thought the place would be deserted."

"That's it." She sat up bolt upright. "Now we only need to find those rats."

She dipped a finger in the now melted ice-cream. Her face took on a dreamy expression. "This is the best. All it needs is a little rose water and it'll be heaven."

In the blinding light of the new day, my new theory still appeared to me simple and plausible.

The two young men wouldn't be the first tourists to be carried away by misguided enthusiasm and a serious lack of judgment. Not that I excused any kind of protest that led to damage, but at least my version of events made it clear that Paolo hadn't been murdered in cold blood.

It didn't bring him back, but maybe it made it a little easier on his loved ones.

"One question, dear partner-in-crime." Adriana sat on the balustrade of the balcony and dangled her legs.

The sun glittered on her blonde hair and her eyes sparkled like the lake in the far distance.

Alive, she would have been worth a fortune as a model for my bespoke creations.

It would have been nice to have inherited her looks as well, but the sad fact was, that at my best moments, a ghost still outshone me without so much as trying.

"Spill," I said magnanimously. I wiped away the last crumbs from my breakfast.

A bread roll, fresh strawberries, and the best caffé latte in Italy on the balcony were a great way to start the day.

Now we were so close to solving the case and hope-fully locating the dress, I felt on top of the world, a sentiment that seemed to be in the air.

In the hotel garden, an elderly gardener trimmed the oleander. He was singing arias in a smooth baritone that would have earned him an audition for any musical talent show.

"If we have fingered the right perps, what are they doing with my Chanel frock?" Adriana asked.

I'd thought about that last night and felt pretty confi-dent I'd hit on the correct answer.

"I don't think they meant to cause a lot of destruction, only enough to cover their trail. They probably snatched a few of the delicate things to save them, or to fund another crusade."

"They should still have it then." She floated down from the balcony. "Unless they have given it to a girl. It's not like the shorter one was a dish, but some girls are swayed by a couple of gems or finery. If anything could do it, my little black dress would do the trick."

"I don't think so, at least not here and not yet. The Chanel frock is very hot right now. If anybody has seen the auction catalog, they might recognize it. My best guess is, it's hidden in a hotel room, or a storage locker at the train station."

She sprinted to the door. "Hot diggity. Then what on earth are we waiting for?"

The streets were busy with cars and motor rollers. I slowly recognized the difference between a honking and quick stops to greet friends chatting on doorsteps, and exasperated honking. I heard snatches of German and French and Dutch, but mostly, the town appeared to be dominated by American tourists.

I weaved my way past window-shoppers and sight-seers, through narrow arches and onto streets lined with wine stores.

Adriana began to weave as well, from one wine tasting tray to the next.

"Stop inhaling alcohol," I told her. "This is not the time to be on the sauce."

She poked out her tongue at me and giggled.

I stamped my foot. "I mean it."

She froze. I stopped as well, only to have a man bump into me without so much as a mumbled sorry.

He was too busy promising the woman clinging to his arm a pampering day at the spa.

Adriana wrinkled her nose.

I gave her a stern look. "What did I just say?"

"Didn't you smell that?"

"I have no idea what you're talking about."

"That woman is using the same hand cream you do. And those two were in the auction house with us. It's the couple who almost hit the pekingese."

Coming towards us, I spotted another familiar face.

I'd last seen it in Livorno, when we bought Adriana's vanity case.

It was the owner of "Yesterday's Treasures" or what it was called, and in her customer powder room I'd first encountered the all important cream.

She spoke in urgent tones to a fortyish man with aquiline features. He wore a bespoke suit and shoes that appeared handmade.

So much for the old adage that all streets lead to Rome. Instead, Montepulciano seemed to be the place to mingle these days.

Adriana stood stock-still. Then she made a quarter turn, and another one. "We're close," she said. "My whole body tingles, and I'm getting goosebumps all over."

"The dress?" I congratulated myself.

We stood only 100 cards away from "Nonna's Albergo", home away from home to our main suspects.

If they had the dress in their possession, it would prove their guilt.

Adriana unfroze and took off so fast I struggled to keep up with her.

Outside "Nonna's", I stopped to catch my breath.

Adriana melted into the wall.

My breath caught in my chest. Please, let her locate the dress, I thought. Then all we had to do was to let Matt and Serina contact the police.

My great-great-aunt made her way back to me with a hangdog expression. "The place is a bust."

"Are you sure?" I bit my tongue. Of course she was.

Yet I wasn't ready to give up.

The walls of the buildings in the old town could have put any medieval dungeon to shame. What if the walls of "Nonna's Albergo" blurred the vibrations or whatever the dress sent out and there was a storage area in an outbuilding?

"I guess we could do a tour," she said when I suggested it.

I scanned our surroundings. Crowded pavements, bistro tables full of tourists, pooches who yapped loudly to impress each other, and aloof cats lounging in door-ways made for a picturesque city.

Adriana drummed her fingertips. "It's driving me crazy. It's somewhere here, I swear. I just can't work out where we should go."

I caught another glimpse of the lady from Livorno and her companion.

On an impulse, I snapped their photo as they walked past the shop where I'd bought the beauty products. "I think I have an idea. Let's follow Ettore's nose."

I picked up the hand cream tester. The sales assistant who bore testament to good genes and the power of cosmetics came close enough for me to engage with her, while still keeping enough distance as not to appear pushy.

"Scusa, excuse me?" I smiled at her.

"What can I help you with?" Her English held only a little accent, which should make my life a lot easier.

"This cream, is it sold everywhere?"

Her features registered shock. "Oh, no. It's locally produced. A small company, with very good products. You will only find it here, and in one bigger store in Florence. It is very exclusive, like most of our products."

I squeezed a dollop onto my hand and rubbed it into my skin.

"Genie." From the other side of a table carrying an artistic arrangement of handmade soaps and flowers, Adriana beckoned me over. "Take a whiff."

I did. And again. I had no idea what she meant.

"Seriously? What's wrong with your nose?"

I gave her a haughty glare. "Some of us have to make do with normal human senses."

"Pardon?" The sales assistant had followed me.

I gave her an innocent stare. "I didn't say anything."

"Smell this." Adriana tapped a bar of soap. I picked it up.

"This is very popular," the sales assistant said. "Gentlemen like that mix of musk and tobacco, it's a throwback to another era."

"I'll take it. You must sell loads of it."

"We do. Our men's products are almost as sought after as the lady's selection."

I winked at Adriana. If we could find Ettore, his olfactory memory might be good enough to tell us if we'd hit the right combination to identify the mystery man, who might well be one of our protesters.

First up though was a tour of "Nonna's Albergo" via the back route.

That's where our luck ran out.

We meandered through the side roads but none lead where we wanted to go.

The closest we came was a café with a hidden garden at the back.

I decided to stop there. I needed water, and a bite to eat wouldn't hurt.

I leant back in my chair when I heard a couple talk. I paid no attention until I caught two familiar words.

They were talking about Odell's Palazzo Vecchio.

I turned around.

Too late, I only saw the man's back and the woman not at all.

"Quick," I told Adriana. "See if you can recognize them."

She sped after them without so much as a single question and returned with the same speed.

She tapped her nose. "We're good. It's the vanity case lady and her companion. They were all gung-ho about taking over a lot of business now the other one was finished."

She settled on the table, next to my drinks. "You know what that means?"

"Our list of serious contenders for villain of the piece just got longer." I drummed my fingers on the table, to help me think. "If only we knew where they're staying. They might be the ones who have your dress."

Chapter Fifteen

hen the receptionist called me on the room phone to announce Matt, I'd prepared an overview of what we knew, what we suspected, and what could have happened.

He arrived with a box of cantuccini studded with almonds and pistachios and a worried expression.

"You shouldn't have," I said at the same instant he said, "Serina sends these. There's a small pastry shop in town that specializes in biscuits."

Adriana, who'd gone all puppy-eyed at his arrival, harrumphed. "Is that the one he's sweet on?"

I gave her a tiny shrug. I hadn't seen anything overly flirtatious at the restaurant, but then the situation didn't exactly scream romance, especially with a third person at dinner.

His next words put Adriana at peace again. "I think she hopes you'll feature them in your food blog. The owners are relations of hers." He put the box on the table. I was flattered by Matt and Serina's faith in my readers who, truth be told, were a tiny group.

"Everything alright here?" he asked.

"Sure." Then it came back to me that I'd used a pretext last night to explain my running away. "Like I thought, it was only a neighbor's cat that got in via the balcony."

"That's a relief. Jolene has given me an earful, about dragging you into this whole business, after you nearly got murdered once already."

"I'm alright, honestly."

I nibbled a biscuit, to prove to Matt how unconcerned I was. "My mother must have spooked Jolene. Ridiculous, but Aimée is prone to a fit of nerves once in a while."

While I spoke I kept my fingers crossed behind my back. Technically I wasn't throwing my parent under the bus. We had a long-standing arrangement that, in certain situations and to dig ourselves out of a hole, we could go so far as to swear on each other's life.

Yet it gave me a sense of unease, to pile up all these lies. I might have to take notes, to keep track of all of them.

"Talking about this whole business, I think we should make a list of possible motives first," I said.

I'd torn a page from my largest sketch book and written down my notes.

Matt read out aloud, "Was Paolo the intended victim and the arson was supposed to act as cover-up? Was it to hide thefts? Or was Tristan Odell behind the whole crime to cash in the insurance money and pay off his debts? Or did a rival try to put him out of business?"

He scratched his nose. "The last idea is new."

"I overheard a man," I said. "This one, to be precise. Have you seen these two before? She runs a vintage shop in Livorno." I showed him the picture I'd taken.

Matt scrutinized it closely, only to shake his head regretfully. "Not me, but Serina might. Can you forward it to me?"

I clicked send, and then I waited. He had to search through his contacts before he found her details.

Adriana gave me the thumbs-up. The glamorous Italian wasn't someone Matt had on speed dial.

"We could send the photo to her," he suggested. "She would be the best person to say if these two have anything to do with the antiques market in this part of the country, aside from selling old knick knacks."

While we waited for a possible reply, he marched around the room. "What I find hard to believe is that anybody would kill a man over these particular objects. It's not as if there was a spectacular masterpiece among them."

Adriana glared at him. Despite her affection for him, she appeared to take it hard to hear her precious little black dress dismissed as unimportant.

"I agree," I said, carefully avoiding Adriana's glare that probably was now leveled at me. "That's why I'm almost sure that our perp didn't mean to hurt anyone. What if he was convinced that the auction rooms were empty?"

To prove my point, I brought up the snapshot of the job ad. "It says, immediate start. It's not hard to see how people could draw the wrong conclusions and believe there was no guard. Even if someone knew about Paolo as an employee, it would be easy to think he'd already fully switched to a day shift."

"That's true. Where is this from?"

"A noticeboard outside a gelateria. I'm sure Tristan Odell would also have put up notices in other places."

I warmed to my theory. "It's also close to where I saw the unknown couple. Plus in the same area I stumbled upon our two protesters who I'm quite sure are at least guilty of attempted vandalism, and some of the folks from the viewing. You remember the blonde woman and her husband?"

I had to pause to catch my breath when another thought made me reconsider my statement. "Was there any sort of alarm system? You did mention cameras?"

If those had simply been switched off, it would point again to an insider job. And who better to steal a dress than the man who had unhindered access?

My eye twitched.

I'd been so sure Odell was innocent.

Now I found myself changing my mind, again.

"The system was the simplest one I've seen in ages, and the camera cable outside was torn off," Matt said. "It could have been anyone though."

"That was the whole security system?"

"That, and Paolo. I'd drawn up a list of suggestions to improve the situation." His face clouded over. "They might have saved Paolo's life."

"There was no way for you to know," I said. We fell silent, until his phone made a welcome noise.

Matt punched the air, in a triumphant gesture. "Yes!"

I waited for him to explain a little further when he gave me a swift hug, only to let go of me with a sheepish look on his face. "Sorry."

"Hey, we're friends, right?" I averted my gaze but I could feel Adriana's romantic notions going on overdrive.

Did people hug for platonic reasons in her era?

I almost missed his next words.

"Of course we're friends, and you are a genius," he said.

Adriana spun around in the air. "Yes, we are," she sang.

"I wouldn't go that far," I said to him. "But feel free to go on. I like compliments."

"Serina has identified the two guys on your picture as a couple with small businesses, dealing in small potatoes antiques. She's a transplant from Ohio, and he's a local from Perugia. They've been trying to capitalize on them having a foot on both sides of the market, so to speak."

That made sense. The foreigners would prefer to deal with one of their own, and so would the locals.

Familiarity went a long way when it came to trust. "They're Tristan Odell's competition?" I guessed.

"More like he was theirs. He had better connections among the foreign community, better taste, and his inventory was much better class. Serina says, with him out of the picture temporarily or permanently, Marisa and Gianluca Galotti had a lot to gain."

"I've been in her shop," I told him. "She had a few items from Lady Taverner's estate."

I tried not to look at Adriana, who was clutching the spiritual copy of the vanity case, if that was the correct term, while I showed Matt the real thing.

Theoretically, I'd accepted the weird duality. Only my eyeballs insisted on swiveling and giving me a headache when I looked too close.

"Why would Marisa sell some parts of it and Odell the rest?" I asked.

Matt examined the damage to the case. "My best guess is, he got first dibs and decided this item wasn't in a good enough shape for an auction. He only sells items under the hammer."

"That makes sense. Just as it would be highly likely that the Galottis have been in Odell's business rooms before and would have first-hand knowledge of his security system or lack thereof." Now I had the urge to hug him, although I resisted. Adriana would only misinterpret it.

"There's only one question. What are they still doing here? Isn't that a little suspicious?"

"Unless there is something going on that would make it more suspicious to leave." His thumbs tapped out a message on his phone at an impressive speed.

Autocorrect must like him, I thought with a pang of envy. On the few occasions when I'd hit send without pausing to check, my texts had ended up as gibberish.

"Can you ask your friend to meet with us? That might be better than all this to-ing and fro-ing," I said.

He looked at his phone and guffawed. "Great minds and all that. Serina just suggested the same thing, if you're up to a spa visit."

My gaze fastened on a glossy brochure on the night stand. Montepulciano, one of the most stunning Etruscan towns on the Tuscan hills, held several claims to fame apart from the eponymous wine.

Movie buffs had seen it on the silver screen in *Twilight: New Moon*, *Under The Tuscan Sun*, *A Midsummer Night's Dream* and other Hollywood hits.

I couldn't say for sure if, in their rare hours off, the film stars had relaxed in the five star spa in town, but I supposed it was likely.

The offerings listed in the brochure were staggering.

So were the prices.

"Don't worry, it's not that one," Matt said as he leafed through the pages and reached the price list. "There's a less insanely expensive one in Chianciano Terme. I could drop you off and pick you up?"

It took me less than five minutes to pack sun screen, my best swimsuit, the fluffiest hotel towel, and the bathrobe in a beach bag.

"Get a wiggle on," my great-great-aunt said, snapping her fingers impatiently.

I flounced out of the door. It would have been more impressive if I hadn't had to return after a few steps to pick up my phone.

Adriana enjoyed the short ride in Matt's rental Lancia, inspecting her image in the rearview mirror. She pouted, blew up her cheeks and rolled her eyes in every manner she'd seen during our movie nights, to give me yet another unasked for lesson in the arts of flirtation.

I made a silent note to really make sure I stuck to classic pictures instead of modern blockbusters.

I didn't mind if Adriana imitated Constance Bennett, Claudette Colbert, or Myrna Loy as Nora Charles, who had lately become Adriana's role model as sleuth.

At least these heroines were on the whole a lot smarter and exciting than the pictures let women be in more liberated ages. And they could dazzle while being fully dressed.

The same could not be said at the thermal baths.

Dipping in and out of the warm open-air pools were an array of women. Some of them would have turned heads everywhere, and for more reasons than their skimpy bikinis. There must be something in their genes that made pizza and pasta slimming, genes that eluded me.

I normally didn't mind. I'd never bought into the idea that five pounds less or a new lipstick were all that was needed to change a woman's life.

Nevertheless I felt self-conscious as I approached Serina who rested on a sun lounger, her face shaded by a wide-brimmed hat.

Next to her lay one of the compulsory bath caps we all had to wear in the water. Hers was a designer affair, which would leave her hair all sleek and stylish. The one I'd been given for a fee at the entrance sported pink and white block stripes and made me look as if I wore an umbrella on my head.

Since I was not floating in the pool right now, I whipped it off.

"She's a looker alright," Adriana said.

"Thanks for --" I broke off and hid behind a man built like a wrestler, with glistening muscles on top of more muscles.

"What's up?" Adriana enquired.

"See for yourself." She did, or at least she disappeared on the other side of my human shield.

Then I saw her hand pop out, stopping me from taking another step.

"It's them," she said. "The folks from the auction house, and your Serina is acting mighty chummy with them."

I withdrew even further. "Can you go and eavesdrop?"

"On my way." She flitted along, and I crept behind as close to our prey as I could while staying under cover.

I really wanted to get an insight into the conversation between the glamorous appraiser and the Stones. But since I'd left the brick from home behind, Adriana had a much shorter range until she became torn every which way.

I moved, only to dart back when Muscle Man threw himself onto a chair that groaned under the load.

Silently I prayed that Serina and her friends would give up the intel fast, before I had to come out in the open.

Although she was expecting me, so I had a reason to be there, I bet the three would not divulge anything of importance in my presence.

My stomach tensed.

How much had Matt and I already given away?

And how could we have overlooked Serina on our list of suspects?

She was the one person best equipped to land a coup and move stolen merchandise, even if her clients only consisted of mid-list players.

Chapter Sixteen

Adriana flitted back to me. In her excitement she slipped back into slang probably never uttered outside Speakeasies and mob meetings in her pulp fiction magazines. "Hold on to your horses. I think we're about to crack this case wide open, and this dame looks fishier than all the cods in Boston harbor."

She held out her hand for a high five.

I was just about to hit it, when I realized mid-motion how insane it would appear to anyone around me if I smacked nothing but thin air.

Also, naturally Serina chose this precise moment to spot me. She waved with a languid grace that caused Adriana to imitate it, again and again.

I plastered a bright smile on my face as I trotted over to the pool.

The water rippled softly in the light breeze, and I could almost feel the benefits of soaking in the warm thermal water. Alas, sleuthing duties came first.

"Have you met Mr and Mrs Stone yet?"

I made a grimace that showed them they seemed familiar, but I couldn't quite place them.

A hairy hand grabbed mine and pumped it with fervor. "Call me Paul, and my beautiful wife is Beatriz. You were at Odell's place, right? I never forget a pretty face."

Beatriz gave me a finger wave that changed into a swat. "Silly mosquito. They're everywhere."

"I've been spared so far," I said.

"Look who it is." Another couple joined us.

It took only one glance at the blonde in a tiny bikini, who snuggled into the arm of her paunchy companion, to make Adriana spit, or at least do her version of spitting. She'd never forgive the couple for the pekingese incident.

Only I was spared from the sudden drop in temperature that my great-great-aunt had by now perfected to show her annoyance.

Adriana threw back her head in triumph as, for a few seconds, she caused goosebumps to appear on naked arms.

"How lovely we're all here." Serina patted a seat next to her. "You've all met, I assume."

"Yes, we have." Once more, my hand was grabbed and pumped.

In a competition, the two men would have ended in a neck-to-neck race.

They mirrored their expensive ladies who covertly scanned each other after dismissing me with a single glance. "Fred Schmitt, and my lovely wife, Lisa."

"Schmitt? I'd say they rhyme with that name," Adriana muttered.

"German?" I hazarded a guess.

"From Munich, but I spent my senior high schools years in England."

His wife interrupted. "We're planning to buy a second home here somewhere. Lake Como has become a little crowded with busloads of tourists hoping to glimpse a Hollywood star."

She gave a little shudder to demonstrate how horrible that scenario must be.

Her husband patted her arm. "We were hoping to pick up a few things already at the auction. Lisa adores antiquities, don't you, darling?"

"And she has excellent taste and judgment," Serina said.

Lisa fluffed her beach-wavy hair. The bath cap that her husband held for her was a stylish turban. So was Beatriz's.

Maybe I should check out if I could buy one of those caps for myself. The white and pink number did nothing for my beauty.

"It's so awful what happened. I can't believe all those lovely things are gone. We rely on you to tell us where to search next," Lisa said.

Beatriz clutched her chest. "I was devastated. I'm very sensitive."

"Me too." Lisa copied her.

Adriana sniggered at the display but I thought I detected real strain in Lisa's face.

"I hope you're not going to be our competition." Fred bared his slightly crooked teeth at me. "You must excuse my memory, but your name escapes me."

"Geneviève Darling, or rather, Genie. And there's no need to worry about me, I was only interested in a few specific items, for friends or rather their small museum back home."

I let that information sink in, before I added, "It's so sad to think the poor guard didn't get out."

"Maybe he was too old to move fast. I've seen so many pensioners here still working in the stores when they should be sitting in the sun and enjoying their retirement years." Lisa's forehead wrinkled as much as her botox treatments allowed.

"If you can call that working. All I've seen them do fast is wag their tongues," Paul said.

"I wouldn't have called him old. He can't have been more than 50," I said.

I could sense Adriana preparing for another chilly spell, until I signaled her to stop it.

I didn't want these people to flee into the warm water, or the indoor area.

"I can't say I noticed him," Beatriz said with a flat tone.

"Not even when he removed those two young guys screaming bloody murder?" I asked.

Paul gave her a look of pure adoration. "I bet you were totally in the zone, honey, thinking about our collection." He stroked her shoulder. "This girl has the best judgment you've ever seen."

"What about your own objects?" I asked. "It must have been a terrible blow."

A shadow crossed his face. "We've decided not to dwell on it. It's sad that they're gone, but there's no real harm done, thanks to the insurance."

"Apart from Paolo," Serina said.

Fred and Paul stared at her blankly while the women had the decency to flinch.

"The guard," she said.

"Poor man." Paul shook his head. "I hope they catch whoever is responsible." He lowered his voice. "I've heard the owner was behind it. He seemed such a nice guy but you can never tell, that's for sure."

Beatriz handed him her bag. Adriana ogled it. "I think she has our hand cream," she said. She wasn't the only one. I was transfixed by what I saw in Lisa's beach tote - an orange blossom body lotion, as sold only in one shop in Montepulciano and one in Florence.

"It was lovely meeting you all," Lisa said. "Maybe we'll see you later, after my musical treatment?"

"You've booked the Sensory Salon too?" Beatriz linked arms with her husband as she stepped into high-heeled mules. "We simply swear by the calidarium."

"You hear that, Fred? We have to try it," Lisa said.

With that, they were off, in the direction of the spa building.

Serina quirked an eyebrow. "And just like that, they're bosom buddies."

"Funny running into each other like this." I giggled to make it clear how funny it was.

"I arranged it." She rolled her shoulders. "I could do with a massage. I hope they're not fully booked for to-day."

"You set up the meeting?"

Adriana gave me a portent nod. "She's in it, up to her neck," she hissed.

Serina said, "It seemed the best way. The Stones had asked for a chat when they heard from our office man-ager I was coming, and I didn't want to give up my visit to the thermal pools before I head home."

That sounded plausible. "And the Schmitts?"

"The men ran into each other, I believe." She made a face. "It's rare that I have the opportunity for self-care."

"Always on the go?"

"You have no idea how many smaller galleries and auction houses there are in Italy. Some offer incredible objects for sale, things that should be sitting in a museum."

"Did Tristan Odell have anything in this category?" I kept my tone light, to show it only asked because of idle curiosity.

"Nice trap," Adriana said. "I bet she'll fall into it."

The roof of my mouth went dry as I waited for Serina's answer.

"It's possible, although it would have to have been a new development for him," she said. "All I ever got to see was the catalog, and a few photos before and after the fire. The problem is, you can't be sure unless you've seen it for yourself and done a few tests."

"How about the Galottis? I assume you're at least fleetingly acquainted with everybody in the business."

"I wish. I can't claim to have an in with the top tier players at the Uffizi but the smaller ones, sure." She wrinkled her forehead. "You think they might be involved?"

I wondered how much to tell her. "I believe it's more likely they would have been able to disable the camera and know the vulnerable spots. I can see a couple of young misguided idealists take care of the security camera, but it would have been risky for them to do anything without knowing the lay of the land. And one quick visit wouldn't tell them what security Odell used. I assume there was a break-in?"

"Those reports are still in progress," she said. "All I have been told with a certain degree of reliability is that the fire was started by an accelerant in the vicinity of the glass cabinets with the jewelry and the dresses."

"Who noticed the fire first? Was it Tristan Odell? He lives at the back of the palazzo, right?" I wondered if she'd give me the same answer as Matt had done.

"He was second on the scene, coming home from an evening in Florence. The alarm was raised by a couple next door."

"That makes it likely that whoever set the fire knew Tristan Odell would be gone."

"Maybe. There is a heavy fire door between the auction house part and the private rooms, and Tristan Odell used to wear ear plugs to keep out any noise."

Adriana and I exchanged a satisfied glance. "That's another thing a stranger would not have been aware of, while the Galottis might have heard the story, and they'd be familiar with the local architecture."

"Tristan Odell and his ear plugs were a bit of an insider joke in the business. I think he might have started telling it himself. It made him appear a little silly, and easier to underestimate as a competition, I was told. Personally, I think it's weird to talk about this kind of personal stuff." She checked her smartwatch. "If you have any more questions or thoughts, will you message me? My train leaves in two hours."

I'd declined Matt's offer to pick us up again.

Like Serina, I rarely had a chance to pamper myself, so I scheduled a taxi with enough leeway for a dip in the pools that had once been a favored haunt of the Romans.

The water felt soft and invigorating enough to make me wish we could stay all day instead of only for a brief visit.

I'd make up for it with another trip, as soon as we had finished our mission. The Sensory Salon that was advertised as a combination of architecture and chakras offering an enticing array of experiences sounded too good to miss, even if neither Adriana nor I fully understood that sentence in the brochure.

When we climbed into the taxi, Adriana sprawled all over the back seat. "Dollars to donuts we were wrong when we suspected Serina, but I'm glad we snapped up my vanity case before the Galottis land in the slammer."

I agreed wholeheartedly. Now all we needed was the evidence.

CHAPTER SEVENTEEN

"Holy moly." Adriana shot upright on the back seat.

"Ouch." I'd craned my neck as the result of her exclamation, so hard that it hurt.

The taxi driver slammed on the brakes. "Signora?"

"It's nothing. Va bene, va bene," I said while I rubbed the affected area.

Adriana leant over my shoulder. For a heartbeat, her shoulder and the taxi driver's appeared to merge, until I shaded my eyes.

"Not now," I whispered.

The corners of her mouth turned downwards as she fell silent long enough for me to relax a little.

We sped up to the hotel room.

Adriana flung herself dramatically onto the bed. "Brace yourself, Genie, because this will knock your socks off."

I pulled up a chair to sit beside her.

"I didn't figure it out, not right away." She propped herself up on an elbow. "Then it hit me like a ton of bricks."

"Wow." Similar to a word like interesting, wow had the advantage of it making no difference if I understand what she was driving at or not, as in this case.

"You say it. Because, bang, it was back." Her excited smile could have lit up the whole room if it weren't already flooded with sunlight.

"It was back?"

"My dress. I had a weird feeling at that spa, and boom, in the taxi I got goosebumps and it was like warm liquid filling my tummy."

For someone who'd technically not been alive since late 1929, her sensations were surprisingly visceral. They were also useful.

I tried to work out exactly when she'd cried out.

It had definitely been past the halfway mark.

If she was right and my calculations proved to be remotely correct, the dress had to be in Montepulciano or at least within less than a five mile radius.

I fired off a message to Serina.

If we were lucky, we should be able to pay the Galottis a visit.

That should establish once and for all if they currently had in their possession a Chanel frock that should no longer exist.

Even if they weren't home, Adriana's ability to sense the garment was proof enough for me.

The one snag in our plan was the little issue that technically the dress could be considered evidence. That meant it could well end up in a police storeroom, but I decided not to mention that now.

First, we had to make sure we could locate it. Afterwards, all we could hope for was that the light-fingered couple had helped themselves to more condemning items, so there was enough evidence left to have them convicted for Paolo's death.

Once we could be sure of that, I would come up with a foolproof plan to keep my promise.

How hard could it be to steal one valuable piece of fashion history?

In my mind I heard my great-great-aunt answer that question. There could be little doubt, she'd declare it with the greatest conviction to be duck soup, or in the more modern terms she'd grown fond of, a piece of cake.

A message arrived.

"Yes!" I exclaimed.

Things were falling into place with reassuring ease. Serina had sent me the address of a hotel where the Galottis had stayed the last time she'd encountered them, before an estate sale in Montepulciano.

I slapped on a sun hat and shades, so I wouldn't be identified so easily, and my ghost and I set out to embark on a little light crime.

Outside, Adriana ran her hand over the handlebar of our Vespa. "Are you sure you want to leg it all across town?"

I'd been wondering the same thing.

Then again, maneuvering the sleek machine along narrow alleys while dodging cars, bicycles and people on foot took its toll.

"We'll go for another ride in the countryside soon," I told her. "I don't want to risk an accident while we're hot on the trail. We'll go straight to the address Serina gave me."

We were less than a mile away from the Galotti's hotel, when we ran into Matt.

He stood in front of a hat maker's shop window, pretending to peer inside.

"What's it going to be?" I asked him. "A handwoven straw Fedora or do you have your heart set on that flat cap?"

He spun around so fast, he threw me off balance.

"Steady there," Adriana said. "Tell him to go with the Fedora. It'll add some cute to his style." She stretched to swipe a curl of hair into Matt's forehead.

My mouth fell open as a tiny strand really moved, touched for real by her spectral hand.

He wiped the hair back. "It is warm today."

Adriana danced around him until I signaled her to stop.

"We don't want to keep you," I hastened to tell Matt.

"We?" He peeked around.

"I mean, I."

"Actually, I was on my way to see you."

"You were?"

"Until I spotted them." He nodded towards the window.

I had to look closely, until I understood.

The glass reflected parts of a bar with a covered patio in a sideway street.

On one of the tables sat our protesters.

"Follow me and don't let them leave." I didn't wait for his reply and sashayed towards the duo.

With a wide smile, I pulled up a chair from their table. "Do you mind, gentlemen?"

They exchanged a quick glance. "You're welcome," the taller one said.

He held my gaze a little longer than necessary, in a flattering way. He definitely was the charmer among the two.

"Thank you - what did you say your name was? I'm Genie, by the way." I sat down the back, with the purse including the brick next to me.

"Smile harder," Adriana whispered. "We don't want them to think you're a bit long in the tooth for them."

Matt stood close by, reading the menu.

The tall guy said, "That's a beautiful name. I'm Willem, and my friend is Hans." There definitely was a hint of flirtation in his voice. He probably thought of himself as a ladies' man.

Hans gulped. Maybe their kind of activism and having a private life didn't mix well for him.

"So, Willem, is there anything you can recommend?" I asked.

"The local beers are good."

Adriana made a gagging noise. She disliked beer.

I waved at the waiter. "A violet spritz, please."

My cocktail came with commendable swiftness.

I took a leisurely sip and put it so my companion could help herself to a noseful. She'd been restrained enough since our arrival.

I stirred the drink and gave Matt a signal to keep himself ready.

"How do you like Montepulciano?" I removed my hat. Adriana mimed fluffing my curls. I did as instructed.

Recognition still eluded Willem and Hans.

I took off my shades too. "Threatened anyone lately or thrown rocks into windows?"

Their metal chairs scraped over the pavement.

"Not so fast," Matt said. He positions himself at my side, effectively blocking in Willem and Hans.

Hans' Adam's apple bobbed up and down. "We didn't do anything."

"There are witnesses," I said.

"You have no right to question us." Willem was made of sterner stuff than his friend.

"That's true," I said. "If you prefer to talk to the Italian police about arson and murder, you're absolutely entitled to do so."

If an Adam's apple could explode, Hans was a prime candidate.

Willem showed first signs of cracking too. His hands clenched. "I have no idea what you're talking bout."

"It's simple." My voice could have cut glass. I'd decided to play the bad cop in this scenario and hoped Matt would be smart enough to go along. "Like I said, there are witnesses who can place you at the crime scene, with rocks in your hands. This isn't a petty crime or a misguided prank. A man is dead."

Matt took over. "If there's anything you have to say in your favor, I'd advise you to do it. We want to help you, if you deserve it. But once the police are onto you, it'll be a lot harder for you to stay out of prison."

I took another sip of my spritz. That drink had a refreshing bite to it. "If you confess now it might just save your skin."

"We went back to the auction house after midnight," Willem said. "We'd thought, we could leave a message to the world about what's going on with looted treasures."

"Like, spray some graffiti," Hans said. "It's been done before and it works, okay?"

"But you didn't," I said.

"The nozzle of the paint can was clogged. So, we picked up a couple of rocks from the garden next door. We didn't even take proper aim." Hans swallowed hard. "We'd had a couple of beers too many, and when we hit a window and heard somebody, we ran. That's all we did, you have to believe me."

For a second I thought I detected a curious expression on Willem's face.

"What about the guard?" Matt pressed them. "It's a lot of coincidence to believe your little vandalism happened at around the same time he was locked into his chamber and the auction rooms were set on fire."

"I don't know," Hans said. "We don't know. We simply ran."

"Okay, let's say for now we believe you. But if you should leave town without my permission, I will send the police after you," Matt said with relish.

"Who do you think you are, that you can threaten us?" Willem had regained his cool.

"Someone who can easily send the carabinieri your way, if you don't listen to me," Matt said.

"How can we bet sure we can trust you? Who are you anyway?"

Matt showed them his business card. "I'm in constant contact with the insurance guys, and the police."

"And you're still on camera from the incident at the viewing," I added for good measure. "Whatever you do, you can't hide."

For good measure I took another relaxed sip.

Playing bad cop had its appeal.

We let them leave and stew over the development.

"That was wizard," Adriana swayed a bit.

The hem of her dress became a little diffuse and the sleeves appeared frayed. She bent over my cocktail.

"Stop," I hissed and lifted the glass away from her.

"Excuse me?" Matt raised his eyebrows at me.

"Nothing."

Adriana tried to grab the cocktail.

I moved it out of her reach.

"One tiny sip of drinky-poo."

Great, now her speech slurred too. I shook my head and glared at her.

"Genie, what's going on?"

Nothing at all, Matt, apart from the fact that I'm fighting a sizzled ghost over a violet spritz, I thought. Out loud I said, "It's the mosquitoes, they drive me insane. I thought they're attracted to blood, but all these buggers want is booze."

I slapped down a ten euro note to pay for my drink. "See you later."

I bolted around the corner.

Adriana swirled and swirled around me like a demented ballerina.

"I said, stop it, before you make me do things I can't explain away and somebody breaks out the straitjacket," I said.

"You're sore at me. I thought we were having fun."

"We are, only not in public."

"It was only Matt and he adores you. No need for you to be such a drag."

"I'm not - forget it. Let's go and wait until you're sober enough to take this seriously. Or we can have another drink and watch you become all foggy. Watch your arms."

She flapped them in front of her and shrieked. "I'm blurred. You've got to help me."

"That's what I'm trying." I jerked my head at her, only to see Matt mirrored in a shop window.

He stood right behind me.

"Genie?"

I'd run out of excuses. "Yes?"

He pressed a bottle into my hand. "Mosquito spray. It's supposed to last up to two hours."

"Thanks."

Soft singing made it clear that Adriana had no intention to shut up. She crooned at Matt and me, "You do something to me."

I fled, for once not caring what my great-great-aunt was doing exactly. Apart from singing into my ear.

Cole Porter would have enjoyed her performance.

I didn't.

Adriana was still going strong when we arrived in our room. She sank onto the bad and rolled onto her front. With her chin propped into her hands and her legs swinging, she crooned. "You do something to me ..."

"No, you do something to us." I flopped next to her onto the bed. "I can't think when you're caterwauling."

"Excuse me? I used to be the star soprano in our school choir."

She kicked me in a playful manner. It felt like being brushed by a blade of grass. I studied her closer.

She was back to her fully formed self. The alcohol and with it, the diffuseness must have worn off. Maybe now we could do what we'd set out for.

The Galottis stayed at a luxury hotel where centuries of history had added to a hefty price tag.

Adriana agreed with me that business either was booming - after all, I'd shelled out several hundred euros for the all-important vanity case - or Marisa and her husband expected a tidy bit of money coming in.

Either way, splurging on one of the most expensive hotels in town cemented their spot on top of our suspect list.

Adriana darted back and forth outside the cream colored building.

I crossed my fingers that it would work.

It didn't. "There's not the tiniest tingle." My great-great-aunt hung her head.

"We did say it's unlikely they keep stolen goods where the maid can stumble upon them," I said.

"I guess so." Still, everything about her drooped. "What now?"

"Now we go for a ride."

I should have thought about it sooner, I decided as I steered the Vespa towards the scene of the crime.

If Marisa and Gianluca Galotti were our birds, they must have used a car or motorbike to get to the auction house. Even if they'd left their getaway vehicle a street or two further away, in a residential neighborhood there was always someone noticing. Especially when it came to nocturnal creatures.

Already the sun had set, and the street lamps were few and far between.

One of them shone into a garden, where Ettore slept under a gazebo.

"We should bring him a bone one day," Adriana said.

"Better not." Maybe in her youth people trusted each other. In these days, I wouldn't put to past them to suspect us of trying to poison the dog.

A cat shot out between two closely parked cars.

"Careful," I called out to it. Or rather, him.

I recognized Pirate Cat who greeted us with a huge yawn.

"Can you translate and let me listen in?" I asked Adriana.

"Fire away." She clasped my hand. It felt like a soft caress.

"Ask him if he saw a vehicle that doesn't belong here in the night of the fire. It would hopefully have arrived shortly before he spotted Willem and Hans and chased them."

Pirate Cat licked his leg as he listened. "I chased them good, oh, I chased them good. There was one big macchina blocking the road, just where the butcher put out his food bins." A fleck of drool appeared on his chin. "That macchina had no business there, none at all, and I would have made sure the humans would understand, if not for the chase." He paused to wash his face. "And then, when I return to my duties as capo of this whole quarter, the big macchina was gone."

"That's awesome. Can he show us where?" I asked.

Adriana made soft noises at the back of her throat.

With a tiny shrug Pirate cat led us to a spot at the corner of a street.

Adriana swayed a little.

I let go of her hand.

"That's odd. He says it had big round eyes." She face-palmed. "I get it. He means round headlights."

"Which limits the range of car models. Better yet, all these houses have signs saying there's video surveillance around here. Tell Pirate Cat he's brilliant."

"He already knows that." She listened for an instant. "He also says he loves fresh fish. The one from the lakes is the best, but he'll accept other fish too."

"Tomorrow," I said.

A question formed in my mind. "How did he keep up with Willem and Hans?"

Adriana chirped at Pirate Cat. He growled in response.

"That's weird," she said. "He says he took a jump, and then he was flying on a bee."

"Crazy," I admitted. "But then he sees things very different from us, I presume."

Realization struck when I caught sight of the old three-wheeled Ape50. I pointed at it. "There's the bee. It's the translation of the name. He must have caught a ride in the open back."

Pirate Cat put his paw against Adriana's hand and purred.

I tried to gather the nerve to ask him if he counted many ghosts among his friends or how he saw her.

While I still pondered the correct phrasing, he took off like a, well, a scalded cat, only to slow his sprint to an amble 50 yards further down the street.

Adriana sniggered. "He's seen an old flame. So sweet how he wants to impress her."

I saw her slip her arm through mine. "Listen to this."

"Are you sure you can handle the strain?"

She rolled her eyes at me.

Together, we listened to Pirate Cat charming a dainty tortoiseshell cat. "Your eyes are like the jelly in the butcher's window, your fur is like the scales on a fresh trout ..."

Grinning, we slipped away, to allow Pirate Cat to court the tortoiseshell kitty in private.

"Where do we go now? Do you think my dress is hidden in their getaway car?" Adriana asked.

"I don't see why not. I'm sure Matt will be able to help us out with the registration number, and then we can search the public parking garages."

"First thing in the morning?"

"I need to sleep, remember? We'll go out right after breakfast."

She whooped with joy, jumped onto the Vespa and leant over my shoulders to grab the handlebars with me. "I wish my mom could see me. She loved her Harley Davidson."

"I can imagine." Rosalind Darling, aptly nicknamed "Daredevil", had scandalized many a respectable citizen of Cobblewood Cove with her outspoken support for the suffragettes, risky flights in double-deckers piloted by her female friends, and her passion for her motorbike.

Old newspaper clippings and photos of Rosalind in her flying uniform and with her motorbike gloves were among Adriana's most treasured possessions.

Nothing though equalled the flying goggles which we'd retrieved from the Cobblewood Cove museum, with the assistance of Matt and a few well-spun white lies.

"I can't wait for tomorrow," Adriana said. "It'll all be over then."

She was right, only not in the sense we both thought.

For in the morning, while I fueled up with caffeine for the excitement ahead, Matt came to break some scary news.

A tourist had been discovered at the bottom of a hill, with a broken neck. He was supposed to have climbed onto the walls, lost his footing and smashed into a tree stump.

The theory sounded plausible enough, except for one thing.

The dead man was Willem.

"Whatever the police believe, Hans is sure they're wrong," Matt said. "He told me Willem went out last night, to figure out something our conversation had triggered. That's the last time Hans saw him alive."

A chill washed over me.

What had we stumbled into that led to the death of two men?

CHAPTER EIGHTEEN

"Another murder." I moved closer to Adriana, who shivered.

"Unless it really was an accident." Matt's voice lacked conviction.

"Not likely, is it?" I said. "What was it they told us, they'd heard another person and ran?"

Matt gaped at me. "You believe Willem went to confront a killer? He didn't strike me as that stupid."

"Hah. That one was a cocky as they come," Adriana said. "The way he strutted about when he was causing a ruckus? And he checked out the ladies, too, all the while. Clear as mud to me."

"What if it was someone he didn't take seriously?" I mused. "Or it could have been a wrong move that gave him away, like searching for a car."

"Are you trying to make him work everything out for himself? Go on and tell him," Adriana said. She was right.

"I think if the police would check all the private surveillance cameras in the vicinity of Odell's palazzo, they'll see the vehicle our perp used. It's probably rented rather than stolen," I said.

Adriana gave me an encouraging nod.

I continued. "It's so obvious, in hindsight. I wonder why the investigators haven't come to that conclusion."

"Oh, they have." Matt averted his gaze. "There's only one hitch. All those signs for video surveillance? At last ninety percent or them are just for show. There was nothing they could check."

"I see." The last bit of hope seeped away. "And I assume there's no chance of establishing if any of our suspects had rented a vehicle?"

"What would be the point? Every second tourist rents a car. It doesn't prove anything."

Since I could barely tell him that right beside him lounged the ghostly equivalent of a sniffer dog, with the ability to locate everything that had once been hers, I fell silent for an instant.

"Where is Hans now?"

If I asked him the right questions, maybe he gave us another clue.

"He's packed Willem's belongings and left."

I goggled, and so did Adriana. "For the Netherlands? Doesn't that strike you as odd, if he' s convinced his friend was murdered? And would the police really let him go just like that? Surely there must be more of an investigation than a quick look before they can close a case? How could anyone decide in five minutes that a death was accidental?"

"You don't mean Hans had something to do with it?"

"I've no idea," I admitted. "But isn't the big question how Willem could so easily get in touch with the killer or at least suss out where to find him? Hans struck me as the type who'd be easy to outsmart. Anybody could pump him for information if he made it seem natural."

"Or she. I bet it was a woman who made a mug out of him," Adriana said.

"Or a her," I said to Matt. "Hans would be used to being overlooked, and archaeology or art history aren't the study subjects that pull in the ladies in droves."

"I minored in art history, and I couldn't really complain." Matt had a twinkle in his eye.

I was grateful for this attempt to lighten the situation, although I struggled to keep a straight face when I saw my great-great-aunt tickle his chin.

"Anyway, he's only gone to Florence, to be safe, with permission from the police. Serina and I could convince Hans to keep a low profile before the murderer decides he too, poses a risk," Matt said. He fanned himself, in what must have been a reaction to my great-great-aunt.

"Smart move. I still think we should talk to him," I said.

"I can try, but I don't think he'll agree. He's scared, and the idea that more people know where he's hiding could send him over the edge."

"Then you talk to him. Find out if Willem gave him the impression he was going to see a woman."

"A date?"

"Not necessarily. But most men don't take us as a threat, especially ones that are full of themselves."

Matt's lips twitched despite the seriousness of the situation. "I'll try, and I promise, I would never underestimate a woman."

"Good."

I paced around, considering our options.

With Pirate Cat's clue about the car obsolete, we were back to square one. We had to locate the dress if we ever wanted to solve this case, and we had to make sure to be careful.

Paolo and Willem's deaths proved beyond any doubt that we were dealing with a ruthless person.

A killer who'd struck twice would hardly shrink back from a third murder.

Matt gave me a wary look. "I'm the one who dragged you into this, but if we find a real lead, we should hand it over to the professionals. I don't want you to get hurt."

"That's nice. Unnecessary, yet nice." A small chuckle accompanied my words. "I don't plan to stir up a killer who thinks he got away with it. If the official version is it was an accident, he'll believe he outsmarted them."

"You'll leave the active case alone then?"

"Good grief, yes. I will not meddle in Willem's murder case."

"Promise?"

For a man I'd only met not that long ago, Matt could be pretty persistent, and flatteringly concerned.

Unless his cousin had put him up to it.

Jolene had been in almost daily contact with my mother who would be eager to see her only daughter out of harm's way, if possible by hundreds of miles.

"Pinky swear." I stuck out my little finger.

After all, I was speaking the truth.

All I intended to do was lay my hands on a certain fashion garment, and that as stealthily as humanly possible.

If I should happen to reel in a killer, that would simply be a welcome by-catch.

I winked at Adriana, to reassure her that our mission remained unchanged.

She frowned at me.

I winked again, only to find myself face to face with Matt.

I'd forgotten she was only standing between us from my perspective. Stupid me. She'd been trying to warn me.

"I've got a lash in my eye," I said, in an effort to explain myself.

He cupped my chin. "Hold still." He was so close I could feel his breath on my cheek.

I blinked, hard. "It's gone, thank you." I took a step back. "I have to go."

He hesitated a little. "If there's anything you're bothered about or if you want to talk --"

"I'll call you."

Once I'd closed the door behind him, I took a deep breath.

Adriana was better at remembering than me that she was invisible. I had to up my game before we returned home, or I'd soon earn the reputation of being loopy in Cobblewood Cove.

Home. It hit me like a hammer what I'd just thought.

I'd rarely planned further ahead than a year or two when it came to where I lived, although I had spent longer than that sharing an apartment and studio with Jilly.

I glanced at Adriana.

Maybe having permanent roots was a good thing, especially when it came with a real home and just enough family history to keep my great-great-aunt grounded without burdening me with too many expectations.

For now though, Cobblewood Cove had to wait.

We had parking garages to explore.

The good thing about small towns was their walkable size.

The bad thing was, Montepulciano made up for that in navigation problems. Its venerable age had led to a maze of vias and viales.

The GPS on my phone constantly promised me we were on the right track, only to change directions whenever I thought we'd come close.

When the shutters in the shops came down for the long lunch break, I had sweat circles under my armpits, and my tongue stuck to the roof of my mouth.

I needed water, and a better plan.

We'd crossed off exactly one garage, which we'd covered inch by inch, to make sure Adriana had a chance to dig deep within herself for any signs of her dress.

We had established beyond any doubt that she had a connection with things where they were.

We'd never tested if she could also sense where they had been in the not too distant past.

If so, we'd be foolish to ignore the chance that she might sniff out the car in question and thus, give us the clues we needed.

My phone rang while I was swallowing my last bit of prosciutto and melon.

The food went down the wrong way as I answered without so much as glancing at the caller ID. "Hello?"

"Genie? Is anything wrong?"

I coughed to free up my airway. "Jolene? Don't say my mom --"

"Aimée is fine, I only wish she would adopt me. Except that she's drawing up all these plans for the garage, so we can convert it into the perfect workspace for you."

"Help."

Adriana jumped onto my lap and hugged me as tight as she could. "I'll protect you."

"I didn't mean help like that."

"Pardon?" Jolene asked.

"Not you," I said into the phone.

To Adriana I said, "I'll explain later."

"Can you speak up?" Jolene asked.

I mimed zipping my lips to my great-great-aunt and took a deep breath. "Please get my mother to stop. I'm fine with her waving her magic wand in my living space if it makes her happy, but I have very specific ideas about my studio, especially if I'm going to share it with my friend."

Adriana's face registered surprise and hurt. Maybe I should have mentioned Jilly to her.

Jolene chortled. "In that case it would be useful if you could decide if you like any of the design suggestions I've sent you. Decent period furniture at a reasonable price gets snapped up fast, and my contact can't hold things for me forever."

"I'll have a look and let you know," I said.

"If it's about the brackets and other fixings, you can always try to source authentic ones later. If everything were period perfect, you'd have a lot of competition, not to mention insane price tags."

"You're right and I should have given you my answer already."

"No need to worry." She chortled again. "I can imagine Matt is keeping you busy enough, or has he been out-done by one of those gorgeous Italian hunks?"

"What? No." I could feel my cheeks burn.

Adriana giggled.

"What has Matt been saying?" I asked Jolene.

"Only that there's been some kind of trouble, but noth-ing that you're involved in other than in an advisory capacity."

"Exactly. Say hi to my mother." I ended the conversa-tion on a confused note. I wrote myself a message as a reminder to check out all my emails and whatever had come in lately when we were back at the hotel.

Before then we had a few more parking garages to track down.

"This is insane." I cast off my sneakers and flung myself onto the bed. "We must have walked twenty miles and all for nothing. Where's my foot cream?"

I dangled my arm out of the bed in the hope to reach the cream pot on the night stand without having to move any further.

My big toe throbbed like crazy, thanks to stubbing it on a shallow step I'd overlooked.

Alas, the pot was just out of reach.

"Are your feet hurting?"

"They're killing me," I admitted.

Adriana cupped her hands around the pot.

She pushed with all her might. "There you are." Her cheeks bulged from the effort.

My heart skipped a beat. I stared at her and then at my fingers.

I could grab the foot cream.

She'd moved the container far enough for me to pick it up.

"How is that possible?"

"Don't act so surprised. You know well enough I can do tons of things."

"When it's moving something that's as good as weightless and has a connection to you, yes. Not if it's something heavyish that I bought on the ship. My slippers weigh half as much, and moving them less than an inch wore you out."

She flexed her arms. "See this? I feel really strong."

To prove her point, she moved the pot another half inch. "Whoopsie. Almost pushed it off the bedside table."

"When did you last feel this powerful?"

She wrinkled her nose in deep concentration and thought. Then she thought some more.

I almost gave up on ever receiving an answer when she said, "At the viewing and a little after that. Why?"

I took a deep breath. *Please let me be right.* Out loud I said, "What if your powers have increased due to being close to the source?"

"We've been here for days," she said.

I deflated. "That's true." I sighed.

She pushed around the jar again. "What now?"

I was busy searching for an inspiration when my phone rang. One glance at the caller ID made my jaw hit the floor. "Adriana? How did you do that?"

"With my mind." She preened.

"Do it again."

"What's the magic word?" She definitely was a Darling. She had the same steely tenacity disguised by a sweet smile as my mother.

"Pretty please with a cherry on top."

My great-great-aunt waved her hand around. The phone rang, only to be followed by a beep.

"I didn't do that second thing," she said.

"It's okay, I only need to recharge the battery. It takes a couple of hours."

I plugged my phone in when the implication struck me. "What if the dress is close enough to affect you, yet so far it takes a while to charge your powers?"

"You mean I'm like this thing?" She poked at the phone.

"It's all energy waves, in one form or another."

"Then what are you waiting for?" She gave me a palpable nudge.

"For my feet to stop torturing me?" I sat up on the bed and massaged the cream into my soles and the throbbing toe. Something sweet would be good now. Sugar tended to kick my brain into a higher gear.

I held up my sticky fingers and grimaced. "I should have helped myself to a biscotti before I covered my hands in this stuff."

"Never fear."

We both watched with bated breath as Adriana plucked away at the lid of the cookie box.

It came off with a plop, and my great-great-aunt stumbled back.

It took us both a couple of deep breaths before she managed to wrap her hands around a cookie and pick it up. "Now, have a nibble."

"Or you could give me a tissue," I suggested.

With my fingers wiped and the cookie devoured, Adriana's mournful gaze traveled to my sore feet.

"If the dress is so close, I could go and search on my own," she suggested.

"Too dangerous," I said. "We have no idea what happens if you're too far from all the items that literally keep you in shape."

I'd seen her body distort and starting to fade once. It had not been a pretty sight, nor a nice experience for her.

I beckoned her to sit with me. "We've done enough running around already," I said. "How about we sit down and think instead?"

Chapter Nineteen

On a notepad I wrote, What we know. I circled the words.

"That's easy," Adriana said. "First, our goons torched the place and made off with my dress. We might buy into Paolo's death having been unplanned, but bumping off Willem? That took cold blood."

"And planning. It's hard to believe that our activist ran into his killer in a convenient spot by coincidence. From what we've seen there are several places where you could make it appear as if he'd had a bad fall, but only a few where you could be sure to be unobserved when you arrange an accident."

"That's what they think." Adriana practically purred herself. "Even if there's only empty shops or closed bars at night, cats own the streets when the moon comes out, and they'll talk to us."

I could see her embracing the idea of interviewing any four-legged witness we could meet.

Except, I had no intention of being spotted at the scene of Willem's murder.

While I stuck to our idea of retrieving the Chanel frock and making sure the killer paid for his crimes, I also planned on keeping as close to possible to what I'd told Matt.

Deliberately stirring up a murderer was not on the cards for me. Contrary to Adriana, I was only mortal.

"I'm sure if we could only figure out the why, the rest will fall into place." I wrote down Motive and circled it.

"Why take the dress?" I mused. "The damage to the fabric means it won't fetch a fortune, on the black market or elsewhere, and you couldn't risk being seen in it here and have your picture in the papers or on social media give you away."

"What about a private party? When I wore it, there was not a single man whose head I didn't turn." She twirled to a melody only she could hear, lost in a beautiful memory.

"That's an option," I said. "Who do we have who fits into that category?"

"Not Marisa," Adriana decided. "She's pretty enough for her age, but a little on the chubby side for my dress." She put her hands on her slim hips and gave me a probing glance.

"There's nothing wrong with having a normal build." To prove my point, I angled for the cookies.

"And we all love the way you look," Adriana said. "I only meant that Marisa and you wouldn't fit in that dress. Belle couldn't wear it either." Her voice caught a little whenever she mentioned her adored older sister.

I allowed myself to be mollified.

Adriana had grown up in a world without constant fast food and convenience stores, and she'd barely reached her twenties before she left the world of the living. Her juvenile metabolism had never had a chance to change.

She grimaced. "That would mean striking the Galottis off our list."

Now I pulled a face too.

It had seemed such a fitting solution.

They both stood to gain a lot of customers among the well-off foreigners who loved nothing better than dropping money on prestige items for their second or third home in Tuscany.

"If it wasn't them, and it wasn't the protesters, unless we believe that little Hans had it in him to supply his best friend with a Chicago overcoat, where does that leave us?" Adriana marched around and around.

I thought back to the afternoon of the viewing.

Adriana's excitement had been at the forefront of my mind.

But there was more.

In my head, I heard two voices utter in awed unison the magic word, "Chanel".

Two women, both tall and slim enough to fit into the dress, and both likely tempted enough to make sure they owned the dress by hook or by crook.

Or by arson.

"Lisa Schmitt and Beatriz Stone," I said. "Or the respective husbands. They both also fit in with the smells Ettore mentioned."

"The puppy-hitters?" Adriana snarled.

"They did not hit the dog," I corrected her. "You saved it."

"But without me, they could have done so, and they didn't care at all. Anyone who almost kills a puppy is also capable of killing Paolo and Willem."

"Good point. They are certainly callous enough." I settled down next to my great-great-aunt. "We need to pay them a visit."

"You think they have my dress?"

"It's at least a lot likelier than the Galottis keeping stolen goods in their hotel room. If they've put the frock in storage somewhere in town, you might feel it if Lisa and Fred have been in close contact, right?" My voice took on a frantic edge.

Truth be told, I had the impression that the sands of time were running out on us, fast.

If I'd been the culprit, I'd have posted the dress well wrapped in a parcel. Keeping it here made no sense.

That is, until I remembered an experience I'd made in Italy, during my first holiday here.

At a local market I'd purchased hand-crafted belts in butter soft leather and sent two of them to my closest friends. They never arrived.

The Italian post could be tricky if there was the tiniest thing they didn't like about the address or the way it was written.

When I told Adriana, she gave me a vigorous nod.

"Belle said the same when she spent the year at finishing school in Switzerland. She said she went to Italy for the art and the food, and did everything else back where people spoke French or German." She swallowed.

I patted her hand. "We will get her gift to you back. We're so close now."

"Do you really believe that?"

"How can you doubt me?"

She wasn't the only one who'd learnt a few moves from our classic movie sessions, so I tapped my nose in my best conspiratorial manner. "Think about it. Who better to have made the same sad experience with the Italian mail than a couple who lives in Southern Germany and is buying a second home here?"

With a little bit of imagination I could see smoke coming out of her ears. "The dirty rats."

She flexed her biceps and raised her fists. "Just take me to them and I'll make them listen to a symphony of chin music."

"Remember, we have to be careful," I warned her.

Despite being pretty sure that the Schmitts would be unable to do serious harm to Adriana, she had a strong connection to the dress. If the Chanel frock was lost to her, who could tell how she'd react?

As for me, I intended to die of old age and painlessly, one very far away day.

That scenario appealed much more to me than the off-chance of coming back as a ghost like my great-great-aunt, if I got bumped off as the third victim in this case.

A chill crept over my whole body.

We'd be safe, I told myself. Willem's death had spooked me. He'd been so young and sure of himself.

Adriana and I were less cocky and much better prepared.

In any case, I intended to leave a note for Matt, spelling out every step of our deductions.

I'd omit nothing, apart from the fact that my sidekick was a ghost and our witnesses all had fur and four legs.

Those were little details that didn't change anything if I kept them to myself.

"Gird your loins, here we come," I said to buck up my courage.

"Attagirl." Adriana flexed her arms again. "Watch out, punks, the Darling detectives are coming for you."

Chapter Twenty

My plan had been simple. We'd reconnoiter where we first saw the Schmitts and then sneak into their hotel once we could be sure they'd gone out.

Too bad I hadn't considered that reconnoiter and loiter had a lot in common, especially when all we could do was hang around and hope our targets show their faces.

To my added chagrin, the hotel the Schmitts come out of the morning of the infamous puppy incident possessed impressive security.

Instead of being able to sneak into a lift and go up to wherever one's fancy took one, people were forced to inform the concierge about the purpose of a visit.

Only if given the all clear, would the lift conductor then transport any visitors to the correct floor.

It was all very reassuring for people who feared surprise guests, and frustrating for Adriana and me.

I had first hand knowledge of the strict security because we'd attempted to waltz in behind a couple who could have come straight out of a fashion magazine. They'd been turned away ever so politely.

A scruffy individual like me (at least in comparison) stood no chance.

I'd considered asking for the Schmitts, or at least their room number, but without a watertight excuse that might backfire. We were dealing with a ruthless killer - or possibly two if the Schmitts had that kind of close marriage.

Unnecessary risks did not appeal to me.

"Boring," Adriana said as we strolled along the road.

I had to admit she was right.

The lack of shop windows in which to peek also made it harder to disguise our surveillance mission.

All I could come up with was a visit to the one café that allowed at least a partial view of the hotel entrance.

I counted my lucky stars that they offered one free table that combined both the view we needed and a potted plant where I could empty my coffee cup if the Schmitts took too long to make an appearance.

As much as I loved my caffeine, there were limits to how much latte and cappuccino I could drink.

Adriana pressed her nose against the window. "If that ain't - no. False alarm."

"This is useless," I said. "There must be a way to get into that place. It's a fortress up front, but what do we actually know about the back?"

Adriana shrugged. "How should I know? I could sneak around for a quick recce."

I hesitated. So far, I'd resisted the idea of letting her out of my sight in public. Then again, what could really happen to her if I stuck close by?

"Okay," I said. "I will consider --"

"Hold your horses. They're coming out."

She bolted before I could do so much as navigate past other customers and tables.

"Wait," I shouted.

A portly couple in baggy shorts and t-shirts which might as well have the word tourist printed on them, blocked my path. "Why? Is there a problem ahead?" the woman asked, clutching her purse as tightly as she could.

"Do you need help, Miss?" Her companion patted the woman's back while he addressed me.

Meanwhile, I lost Adriana out of my sight.

"My mistake." I faked a cheerful smile. "I thought you were someone else."

"Oh, how exciting," the woman enthused. "Do you hear that, honey, we have doppelgängers in Italy."

"Yes, you have." I pointed in the direction opposite to where I intended to sprint. "Dead ringers. They went down that street."

With that bald-faced lie, I moved past them and after my dear great-great-aunt.

I caught up with her outside a wine shop where a tasting tour was beginning.

"Will you stop lallygagging," Adriana said. "Otherwise we'll lose them."

I followed her gaze. The Schmitts formed the rear of a group following a handsome sommelier down to the cellar.

"Come on," she said.

"No. And you won't go either."

She hiccuped. "And why ever not?"

I motioned her away from the entrance to the shop with its intoxicating fumes. "Because you're already half way to being drunk."

"What a rude thing to say." A sour-faced customer glowered at me.

Once again, I'd overlooked the fact that there might be people behind me, helping themselves to samples, and that my conversation partner was invisible to them.

I mumbled an excuse and fled, hoping that Adriana would follow my lead.

She did, grumbling about spoilsports and missed opportunities.

I tuned her out.

We had only a short period where the coast was most likely clear in the Schmitt's hotel room. Now all we needed was to establish where to go and how to get in.

A liveried bellhop picking up a flower delivery gave me an idea.

Adriana admired the gigantic rose bouquet I chose, which was large enough to hide my face behind. "I haven't been given flowers since my 21st birthday, and roses are my favorites. And orchids, I love orchids."

Since the aforementioned birthday had occurred in 1929, she'd gone flowerless for a long time.

I made a mental note to send us a bouquet once we were safely back home. The roses I held in my hands now served another purpose.

The receptionist in the Schmitt's hotel had the glossy sheen of a woman used to all the beauty treatments available in Montepulciano and vicinity. Her perfectly arched eyebrows and sun-kissed skin with just the right amount of dewy glow and her fitted skirt and silk shirt made me feel plain and underdressed in my jeans.

The wide-brimmed sunhat and mirrored shades I'd purchased to cover me up as much as possible didn't help in the elegance stakes either.

I changed my voice and faked an Australian accent. "Excuse me, somebody made a bloomer. These flowers were dropped off in the wrong place." I put a handwritten card on the marble counter. "See, it says, Lisa Schmitt. That sure isn't me."

She studied the note. "Va bene." A languid wave of her hand, and a bellhop hotfooted it over to us.

"Can you call them? Please?" I angled my head so I caught a glimpse of the phone as she typed in a room number. At least I hoped that was the 357 stood for.

"There is no answer," she declared after half a dozen ringtones.

"That's too bad, mate. I'd hate to come back." A door at the back of the hall swung open and revealed a walled garden.

"We'll take care of it." The receptionist signaled the boy to take the bouquet from me.

"Go," I hissed under my breath as the she told the boy to take the flowers up to the room.

Adriana sashayed towards the lift, and I swiped the card off the counter.

"The note," I exclaimed and pointed downwards.

The receptionist rose and took a look, before she called back the boy. They huddled together for only a few seconds but that was long enough for me to dash through the door to the garden.

I'd rather not be seen by the Schmitts, hanging around outside their hotel while I waited for the return of my sleuthing ghost.

Adriana took so long to reappear that I started to have palpitations.

Twice the door to the walled garden had opened, and a guest had shuffled in, followed by a waiter with a tea trolley. Twice I'd hunkered down in a corner and pulled my sunhat deeper into my forehead.

A gloved hand poking out of the wall was the first hint my great-great-aunt was back. Her head followed.

"Let's scoot," she said before she was gone again.

I strutted out of the hotel, with the air of someone who spent her existence in the lap of luxury. People only saw what they wanted to see, and acting timid would give me away as an imposter.

To my relief, the receptionist had her nose deep in a ledger as I passed her.

I mentally patted myself on the back when I crossed the road outside the hotel and missed running into Lisa Schmitt by a couple of inches.

Chapter Twenty-One

"Someone doesn't look happy," Adriana muttered, although I couldn't tell if she was being sarcastic because her face held the same gloomy expression as the German's.

Lisa Schmitt stumbled blindly past me, with her husband trotting after her.

He ignored me as well.

I shrank back into the shade of a column.

Adriana joined me after a brief detour to trail the Schmitts. "They're jabbering away in German," she complained.

"You can't understand them?" For some reason I'd expected her to be omnilingual, if that was a word. After all, she could talk with animals everywhere.

"No."

"What else do you have to tell me?" I whispered, before people around me called the local psychiatric unit and booked me a place for an indefinite stay.

"It was a bust. They don't have my dress in their suite." She pushed her bottom lip out.

"I'm sorry."

We trudged towards our hotel.

So preoccupied was I with my next metaphorical steps that I didn't watch my literal ones until I slipped. I stumbled down a step that was worn to glassy smoothness.

Only Adriana's quick reaction saved me. She jumped in front of me, to break my fall.

I slowed down enough to be able to slam my hand against a wall, next to a sparkling window which mirrored everything. I saw myself confronted with my astonished grimace, and with Lisa Schmitt. She strutted past like a woman on a mission, and one that did not bode well for her adversary.

"Can you see her husband?" I asked Adriana.

"No." She giggled. "Did I tell you he wears slippers with pompoms? Too funny for words."

She'd obviously recovered from her disappointment.

I hesitated.

If Lisa Schmitt was in on the crime, it could be dangerous to tackle her alone.

Then again, I'd never have another chance to worm a few things out of her.

"Can you go to our room?" I asked Adriana.

"You want to get rid of me." Adriana pouted.

"Of course not."

She crossed her arms.

"I just can't afford to be distracted. You're very hard to ignore. Please? Before I lose Lisa?"

"You better get her to sing like a canary," Adriana told me and sighed. "Okay. If you're sure you can handle her without me."

I was.

I found my target in a bar, ordering a double espresso and ham sandwiches. Every movement of hers was angry, and the waitress kept her distance as she followed Lisa to a table.

I sidled up to her. "Lisa?"

Her head jerked up. "Oh, it's you. I forgot your name."

"Genie." Up close, she seemed more exhausted than angry. Fine lines crisscrossed her forehead, and she swallowed hard.

"Are you okay?" My gaze flitted to the door.

Had she stumbled upon evidence of her husband's misdeeds and tried to decide what she should do?

Would Fred Schmitt come rushing in to stop her?

She took a sip of her espresso and grimaced. "Where's the sugar?"

I handed her two paper sachets from another table.

She poured them both into her black brew, turning it into caffeine-loaded syrup. She drank it without batting an eyelid. "I'm so angry," she said. "Have you ever had this urge to strangle someone because they simply won't listen to you?"

I inched away a little with my chair and waited for her to continue.

"He is such an idiot," she muttered. "I told him I'm not having any more of his behavior. If he wants to end his life, that's fine with me. But hurting others?"

Now I swallowed.

She had found out about her husband's crimes.

"What are you going to do?" I asked as I signaled the waitress to bring us two bottles of water.

"Do? Nothing. What can I do?"

"It must be so hard." I'd almost told her to go to the police, but that was too risky since I had no clue how far she'd go to protect her husband.

"It is. I'd hoped he'd come to his senses, after our last car trip."

She uttered a bitter laugh, confusing me completely.

What on earth was the woman talking about?

"His doctor should have told me," she said. "Imagine a medical professional who knew Fred's eyesight wasn't only too bad to drive at night any longer, but also that my husband shouldn't be allowed behind the wheel at daytime. I had no idea until he almost ran us into a wall. And now Fred talks about hiring a car again and exploring the countryside."

"Your husband has problems with his vision?"

"He's getting worse and worse. It's okay for everyday life, but in a car he's a menace, and he won't let me drive."

"Is that why he almost hit the puppy?"

"He did what?"

"When you were driving off a few days ago. He missed a Pekingese by a few inches."

"That's enough. I'll take his license away from him and burn it before he kills an innocent animal. Or a human." She gulped down water. "Thank you for telling me."

"I'm sorry." I meant it, too.

I felt sorry for her, and for him too. I t must be tough to lose the independence of driving a car. Mostly though I felt sorry for Adriana and me.

If Fred could barely manage a vehicle during the day, there was no chance at all that he'd been able to drive to Odell's auction house, set the fire and make his escape without an accident.

We were fast running out of suspects.

"Thanks for listening." Lisa pushed back her chair. "I should go and see that my husband doesn't do anything stupid, like rent a motorbike."

I watched her as she left in a power walk, no longer as angry, but I wouldn't want to be the one she had a beef with.

Good on her, though.

Adriana jumped off the sofa when I entered. "How did it go?"

"Don't get your hopes up," I told them. "The room search was a bust because the Schmitt's didn't do anything."

"He almost hurt a dog," Adriana said.

"He did, and he couldn't help it. Behind the wheel, Fred is blind as a bat."

"Drat."

"Yes." I flopped onto the bed next to her.

She heaved a sigh. "Yeah, well. There once was a desolate Genie, and Adriana could rival Houdini--"

"Hold that thought." I fished out my phone to make a voice note of her new limerick.

Adriana had once hoped to become a famous author. With her permission I'd read a few of her early poems and stories. They'd been promising, if I were to judge.

Getting back into rhymes might kickstart her second artistic phase and give new meaning to the term ghost writer.

I'd just dictated the opening lines when my phone buzzed, and I read a message from Jolene.

"Still waiting for your decision. Otherwise your mom has a few other ideas up her sleeve."

I'd completely forgotten about the remodeling back home.

I scrolled through the older messages.

There they were, two bulging files full of photos.

"Crunch time," I said to Adriana. "Let's see if any of this could be the interior design of our dreams."

We both fell in love at the same time, with an Art Deco silk screen that cleverly introduced peacock feathers into a geometrical motif.

The same pattern was repeated in a wallpaper that would give the room the correct period feel as a feature wall, especially if paired with the sconces Jolene had mentioned.

I zoomed in to figure out what she'd meant with the wrong fixings.

Then it hit me.

I closed the file.

"What are you doing?" Adriana asked. "I thought this is urgent."

I didn't answer. Instead I typed a quick message to Matt.

I needed the crime scene pictures, to make sure I was on the right path.

He sent them while I mentally rearranged the puzzle pieces we had.

I opened the auction catalog, with the description of the articles, and laid it ready to compare with what I saw.

Adriana put her head next to mine. "What have you found?"

I told her.

"Jeepers," she exclaimed. "Now what? Send in the flat-feet?"

"No. First, we need to find proof."

"I thought we had it right here." She tapped on the phone screen, which became blurry while her energy hit the device.

I rushed to take it away from her. "I'm talking about tangible evidence, something that will put our criminals on the spot in a court of law."

"My dress." A hint of fear crept into her voice.

"Hopefully there'll be more than that, but otherwise it'll have to do."

I felt a pang of guilt as I saw her desolate expression. "There will be a possibility to get it back somehow." I hoped I sounded more convincing than I felt. "It's all I can think of to ensure that Paolo and Willem's murders don't go unsolved."

She perked up. "You've got a plan?"

I looked from her to the phone and back. "Oh yes, and it all depends on you."

CHAPTER TWENTY-TWO

The rental villa stood a little back from the street. It lay in complete darkness, as far as I'd been able to see when we circled it.

Street lamps threw their diffuse beams onto the asphalt.

The lack of a sidewalk made it harder to pose as a woman on a harmless evening stroll.

We doubled back through a side alley and towards a tall pine stand flanking the patio.

A wrought iron garden gate offered easy access to the house. Wisteria climbed up on the pink wall, all the way up to the balcony on the second floor.

The yellow house next door sat conveniently empty, according to the listing on the rental site. I'd chosen the dinner hour for our little trip, to set up the trap we hoped to spring on our villain.

Adriana fizzed with excitement. She whooshed around on air, too preoccupied to put her feet on the ground.

"Are you ready?"

She gave me a disdainful glare. "Sure I am."

"I could come with you to the door," I said.

"No, you stay here while I'm going to knock them for a loop." Clearly, she enjoyed her role as heroine.

Fine with me, as long as she stuck to the plan.

I cowered in the dark, behind a tree, and observed my great-great-aunt melt through the French door and enter the lion's den.

I counted the seconds under my breath, more to distract myself than to collect any sort of useful information.

I had no idea how many rooms there were in the three-story building, although I'd checked the description in the advertisement for rental villas.

The master bedroom with its wall-length wardrobe and enormous dresser was the likeliest hiding place for stolen goods.

There was no regular maid service, but any smart crook would make sure he had the easiest access to his valuables, if things went sideways and he had to stage a premature arrivederci.

Adriana floated down from the balcony.

Her dress shimmered in the dark, and her hair framed her head like a halo.

Something had supercharged her and it didn't take a genius to solve this puzzle. "You found the dress."

"Did I ever! And not only that, you were right on the money about the stuff they've stashed away."

The metal gate in the front squeaked open.

The second act was about to begin.

I itched to be on the spot but since I couldn't make myself invisible, I had to rely on Adriana and on the old adage that the guilty flee where no man pursues.

All I really could do was rattle them good and proper and hope that they'd loose their cool.

I left my hiding spot and ducked behind the neighboring wall. The bricks were laid in an intricate pattern that left enough gaps to peek through while still giving me ample cover.

I saw the lights go on upstairs.

Paul and Beatriz Stone had returned, to a place where a ghost stood ready to haunt them.

My heart beat accelerated to a point where it echoed so loud in my ears that it blurred every other sound.

If only I could be sure that Adriana had been able to slip our carefully prepared note under the door. It had taken us hours to craft it.

For an innocent person, it might be gibberish.

For a murderer, it would tell them the game was up.

I'd written in stenciled letters, "I know what happened. Meet me in the churchyard of Chiesa di Santa Lucia in half an hour and we can discuss the situation."

I'd chosen the baroque church for its slightly remote location and because of the singular front door frame and two empty niches beside them that once had held statues.

It made for a sufficiently sinister place to meet with a prospective blackmailer without being seen. Not that I intended to be there, not by a long shot.

All I planned to do, if they rose to the bait, was to bide my and Adriana's time.

My pulse had settled back into a healthy, steady rhythm when a familiar shape came into view.

My great-great-aunt was back, with a face-splitting grin.

We crouched deeper behind the wall.

"Did it work?" I whispered despite the fact that we were alone.

"Like the pope on Sunday. He's a cool egg alright, I'm telling you, but his wife screeched at him so loud I thought my eardrums would burst."

"And you got it all?"

"Sure I did." She sank against the rough stone, flagging a little after her exertion.

I breathed out a long, calming breath.

Any second now we should see if I'd read the couple correctly or if I'd made a mistake.

Adriana had hidden her phone under the Stone's bed during her first visit. Then, after their return, she'd floated in again and switched it on recording while the couple discussed my little note. The tricky part was that we still had to retrieve it.

Adriana couldn't do it, at least not so soon. She was too exhausted.

That only left me.

"They're coming out," she said in a soft tone.

"Both?" I automatically crossed my fingers. Our whole plan hinged on that fact.

"Joined at the hip."

"Hooray for that." Our gamble had paid off.

I had no doubt that the Stones intended to split up and deal with the blackmailer, just as I had no doubt that Beatriz had acted as decoy to lure out Willem.

Adriana giggled. "We should give ourselves a new name, because you're Genie, and you and me equals us."

I gave her a non-comprehending stare.

"Seriously? Genie? And us?"

I ran that through my mind. "Good grief. Genius."

"Not if your grey cells are working at that speed."

"I'm busy with other things."

We crept closer to the street, where the Stones started their car.

My hands felt clammy. "Run me through it again."

"Second floor, second door on the right, under the bed."

She wrinkled her nose. "Whoever cleans for them has done a lousy job, so don't worry if there's a cobweb or two on your hands. All you need to do is keep your mouth shut if you have to crawl underneath and you'll be peachy."

Her voice was a little too bright. I'd expected her to insist that she'd come with me to collect the phone with the recorded evidence.

She must be drained worse than I'd thought.

I entered the house via a time-honored method, by opening the French doors with a laminated company card from the same car rental the Stones had used.

I thought it was a nice touch.

My rubber soled shoes made as little noise as possible on the marble floor, and I wore gloves to prevent any marks.

As much as I wanted this to be over as fast as possible, I forced myself to take it slow.

I didn't dare switch on the lights, so I only had the illumination from my phone to rely on.

Nevertheless I found the master bedroom without a problem.

A valance covered the large four-poster right down to the mosaic tiles. I knelt next to it and shone the light from bed post to bed post.

There, an arm's length away, lay what I'd come for.

I stretched my arm as far as I could.

My fingertips touched the phone case. I gave another push, and added another inch to my reach until my hand closed over the phone.

I tiptoed down the staircase, when the light in the hallway flooded the entrance.

In an instant I hastened back up, in the desperate hope I'd remained invisible.

My heart hammered painfully in my chest, and I had a hard time controlling my breath.

Maybe I could get away through the bedroom and over the balcony.

Then my phone rang.

I ran, but Paul Stone was fast, too fast for me, and he was strong.

His hand held me in a choking hold before I could make it to the balcony door. Black spots danced in front of my eyes as he pressed harder.

I clawed at his hands, cursing the fact that I wore gloves. They made it impossible for me to properly grip or scratch him.

Think, Genie, *think*. I'd done a self-defense course ages ago.

How did that acronym go? SING. Solarplexus, instep, nose, groin.

"What are you doing here?" Paul snarled.

Instead of an answer, I tried to lift my elbow, but he held me too tightly. So much for solar plexus and nose. I lifted my knee.

Within a heartbeat, he'd pinned me harder against the wall.

I stomped on his foot as hard as I could. He cursed.

"Watch it, you no-good thieving punk," Adriana yelled.

The bulb in the wall sconce burst, sending shards flying towards Paul.

He flinched and loosened his grip.

Adriana send off a blast of cold air, fueled by her rage. While he recoiled, I elbowed him in the guts, karate-chopped him out of my path, and ran for my life.

Despite all this, he was hard on my heels as Adriana and I barreled out of the villa.

Beatriz Stone's jaw dropped as she saw us. She started the car engine, ready to give chase, when her husband jerked the door open and pushed her aside, to take the driver's seat.

He pointed the hood in my direction and floored the pedal.

"Now?" my great-great-aunt asked.

I gave Adriana a weak nod as I threw myself over a gate and into a courtyard.

I watched her punch the air and make a blocking motion.

The engine stalled for a moment, and the car lurched. Adriana swerved an invisible steering wheel. An ugly metal crunch announced that the Stone's pursuit had ended against a tree.

Adriana had successfully caused them to have an accident.

The last I saw of the couple were their hands, fighting inflated airbags.

They were still inside the crashed car when the police and Serina arrived.

Matt couldn't be far behind, if he had received my earlier text message.

I allowed myself a small moment of delayed panic before I sent him a quick reminder to meet me around the corner and collect the phone with the recording.

He was to hand it over to Serina, no questions asked, no questions answered.

He appeared in time to stop me from having a nervous breakdown. There was no scenario in which I'd be able to deal with the Italian police myself and explain how I'd come to be in the possession of this hopefully vital piece of evidence.

Being booked for breaking and entering would not look good on my resumé.

I stopped myself from mentally babbling and resisted the urge to fling myself into Matt's arms as he finally stood before me, all broad shouldered and solidly reliable.

"I'll explain later," I promised as I palmed him the phone.

He quirked an eyebrow at me. "Your place? Otherwise you'd have a long drive ahead, and you look ready to drop."

I saved myself a tart response. Being chased by a twofold killer does not improve a woman's appearance.

Instead, I gave him a brief nod and left it at that.

Adriana blew him a kiss. I could have sworn, he react-
ed with a smile, although that could be due to his relief
that, with any luck, this case should be over.

CHAPTER TWENTY-THREE

Before I could muster the energy to do anything to restore my beauty, I sank onto my bed.

Adriana bustled around.

I could imagine the swishing of her evening gown.

"Aren't you going to ask me anything?" she demanded.

I groaned as I heaved myself up. I needed a caffeine fix, a quick wash, and a brush.

Adriana scanned my black jeans and dark sweatshirt. Both carried visible signs of my encounter with the Tuscan masonry and plant life. "I'll tell you while you make yourself presentable."

I dragged myself over to the coffee machine and switched it on. "I'm all ear."

My great-great-aunt, old Hollywood's greatest loss, draped herself onto a chair and struck an expectant pose.

Only when the coffee machine had finished its job and I sipped my much needed beverage, did she break her silence.

"I was doing the look-out while you went inside, as we'd agreed. A little boring, really, at least in the beginning. I had a chat with a pretty little dog."

I made encouraging noises.

Adriana continued her tale. "Out of nowhere, the automobile returned, and I heard Paul growling in that hoarse voice of his, that the wife better keep it together next time and not forget his peashooter again."

"He forgot a gun?" My mouth went as dry as the Sahara on Midsummer's night as I recalled my lucky escape.

Adriana mimed shooting up the room. "I bet he wanted to make sure you ended up dead as a doornail at the church."

"You hadn't mentioned he had a gun before I went inside." I found it hard to overcome this point.

"I hadn't seen it," she admitted. "I only searched for the things on our list. It's okay anyway, because I saved your bacon, again."

"You did," I admitted. "And Matt and Serina played their part too."

As if on cue, the room phone rang, and a disapproving night manager told me there was a Mr Blake downstairs to see me.

I told him to send the visitor up and, thanks to the caffeine in my blood, was able to sprint to the bathroom to run a brush through my hair.

"You should swoon," Adriana told me as Matt stepped into the room. She demonstrated how she'd buckle to her knees.

"No," I said through closed teeth.

"Men like to rescue a damsel in distress," she said.

I gave her a tiny head-shake. "Take a seat," I told our visitor.

He did. By now I'd become so used to seeing them together that I didn't do so much as bat an eyelid when Adriana perched on the arm of his seat.

"I'm glad you're okay," he said with a concerned inflection. "That was a close shave you had."

"It was."

Adriana fluttered her lashes. "Try it like this."

Stubbornly, I stuck with my normal method of blinking only when necessary.

"How did you discover it was the Stones?" he asked.

"Simple, really, once I put two and two together. We should have realized that, if we discounted Tristan Odell, they were the ones who stood to gain the most from an insurance payout. Beatriz also mentioned an earlier visit during the viewing."

It still smarted how many clues we'd overlooked, but at least in hindsight I could tie them together. "The biggest giveaway, which admittedly I hadn't noticed during the viewing, was that there was something off with their miniature paintings of Napoleon and Josephine's eyes. When I looked closely at the catalog and the crime scene photos, it jumped out at me. "

"Serina said only a handful of people would have spotted that the chains and the clasp on the pendants were wrong. Sh e is not exactly happy with herself that she didn't pay enough attention to the catalog."

I took the compliment in my stride. "It would have stood out to her once she saw the jewelry up close, which is what he couldn't allow. Stone had been smart enough to stick to the correct period, but it was unlikely that, two centuries ago, a British silversmith would have been used by an Italian artist, especially for hand-painted jewelry that only was in fashion for a couple of decades."

I paused, to give Matt the opportunity to be suitably impressed. Then I continued. "Once I thought harder about it, the less likely it appeared that these miniatures were the real deal. Otherwise, why choose a relatively obscure auction house with no high-rollers on the client base? Unless it was exactly for that reason. Tristan Odell had a decent enough reputation, and better still, he took on items at face value. I assume Paul Stone had recent appraisals, and insurance."

"He was clever, but not half as smart as the detecting Darlings." Adriana preened.

Matt nodded. "Whoever he named will be subjected to a rigorous investigation."

"It all would have worked in his favor," I said. "Until you threw a spanner into the works and convinced Tristan Odell to bring in an expert at the last moment. I guess the Stones would have been the first he called, to inform them or maybe to invite them along. That must have clinched it for the couple."

"We believe Paul Stone would have torched the place anyway, to steal his originals back and replace them with copies. The fire started next to the vitrine they were kept in, so he could be sure they'd be severely damages."

"If what he has are originals, which I doubt."

"Not in the sense that they were made for Napoleon Bonaparte, but Serina confirmed they are period pieces alright and would have fetched a few thousand on the black market from a gullible collector. That, together with the insurance sum, would have been worth six figures to him."

He gave me a smile that raised the room temperature a couple of degrees. "You took a huge gamble, and that after your promise to leave well alone."

"I couldn't stop thinking of that poor guard, and of Willem. And I knew you and Serina would act once I sent you a photo of those blasted painted eyes."

Technically speaking, Adriana had taken the picture, empowered by the presence of her dress, but that was an unimportant detail.

"It should be enough proof to lock him up," he said. "She might get away with it, though."

"Applesauce." Adriana blew out her cheeks. "I heard those two and they were in this together right from the start. She's a bad lot."

I grinned at Matt. "I assume the police won't share the recording with us."

"Not likely, I'd assume. Nothing I can do about it."

"Would you instead care to listen to the copy I sent to myself, as a back-up?"

"What a clever woman you are." He relaxed deeper into the armchair opposite mine, unintentionally elbowing Adriana.

I wondered if he'd accidentally made tangible contact, because she left his side to stand undecided between us.

I hit replay.

It started with a promising screech, and a few treacherous words.

"They're on to us."

"Shut up. I need to think."

Adriana and I shared a frown. Lovely, how Paul Stone treated his wife. There really was no honor among thieves and murderers, married or not.

Beatriz hissed at him. "You said it was over. You promised with that student gone ..."

"That doesn't matter now. The question is, where did we screw up?"

An ominous pause.

I held my breath, and Matt leant forward, transfixed on listening.

Adriana grinned to herself.

"It has be the runt he had tagging after him," Paul said.

"We've got to take care of him then," his wife said.

I could practically hear the wheels in Beatriz's brain turn. "Where in tarnation is Chiesa di Santa Lucia? Do you remember that church?"

Paul gave a dirty little laugh. "It's a little out of the way. Perfect for a quiet encounter. You lure him out …"

"You think he'll fall for the fleeing woman trick?"

The hairs on my neck stood up as I heard Beatriz weighing her options.

No lawyer would be able to make that go away.

Paul reassured her. "His friend did, and he was a lot smarter. He doesn't have to buy your act, as long as you distract him for a few moments. I'll do the rest."

"I hate dead bodies. They give me the heebie jeebies."

"Just once more, sweetheart, and then I promise you we're home free."

The recording broke off.

"That's when I legged it," Adriana said. "I told you it's a doozy."

"You can say that again." I shivered.

"What?" Matt knitted his brows.

"At least we can be sure they were both in on this together, from start to finish. That should be enough," I said.

"It should." He gave me a little smile. "And I should be going now. I promised Serina I'd come over for a chat. She has to explain how she came into the possession of a certain phone."

"Right." I chalked up the pang I experienced when he left as hunger. I'd been too on edge earlier to eat much.

Pizza would be nice, or a burger.

Still, my stomach would have to wait. All I had to keep me going until breakfast were a handful of biscotti I could dunk into my coffee, never mind if it kept me awake all night.

I wouldn't be able to catch a wink under any circumstance, not while I had no idea what was going to happen next.

As brilliant as Adriana's and my plan had been, what if I'd not been successful in wiping my fingerprints off the burner phone completely? Worse still, what if the police checked the records of the provider?

After all, I'd purchased the phone and SIM card for Adriana. The police might stumble upon my name. What if they came knocking on my door, as a potential accomplice?

I buried my head in my hands.

That thought alone was enough to keep sleep at bay.

Chapter Twenty-Four

I woke to a clear, sunny, and best of all, police-free day.

The church bells chimed, Adriana danced around the room and all was well with my world - until I counted the chimes.

Eleven! I'd missed the breakfast slot.

On the upside, I only had a couple of bruises to show as a reminder of last night's adventure instead of a bullet hole.

Paul and Beatriz Stone should be safely behind bars, and we were surrounded by one of the most beautiful landscapes on earth, with no danger to life and limb in sight.

With that huge load off my mind, going out for breakfast would be a pleasure and well worth waiting for, rumbling stomach or not.

Adriana rifled through my wardrobe. "You should wear this dress," she said. "It would look spiffing on you."

I couldn't deny her taste. The burnished orange of the silk contrasted nicely with my dark hair, and the fit flattered my curves.

That said, it was also the only evening dress I'd packed and not quite the perfect attire for today's program. "I'll wear it another time. For now, jeans and t-shirt will be fine."

She pouted. "You could do with a little more oomph."

Easy for her to say. She was eternally dressed up to the nines, unwrinkled, crease-free and ethereal.

Others, like me, had to live with a few more restraints.

"Jeans are perfect for taking out the Vespa," I said.

"Goody." Adriana flopped onto the bed and rolled onto her front, chin propped up in her hands. "Where are we going?"

"I thought we'll have breakfast and then we'll pay a visit to Ettore and to Pirate Cat. They deserve to hear the truth, and to receive a treat or two."

I grabbed my clothes and headed for the bathroom.

Ettore dozed in the sun. Adriana crouched next to him and whispered into his ears. His head nodded as he listened.

When she had finished, the old dog pushed himself upright and lumbered over to me and pressed his head against my hand.

"He says thank you."

I patted his back. "You're welcome. Good-bye, Ettore."

Adriana sniggered as a sleek grey kitty ambled up to her and, a split second later, Pirate Cat jumped into view.

The two cats entered a staring contest.

"Help the grey one win," Adriana said. "Now. This is important."

I whipped out the parcel with fresh fish I'd bought and opened it.

Pirate Cat's head swiveled around. He pounced. His stomach mattered more than a staring contest, it seemed.

The other feline gave her face a dainty wash and purred.

Pirate Cat halted mid-chew and stepped aside.

She helped herself to a bite.

He chirped, and Adriana giggled.

She grabbed my head.

Again, we heard Pirate Cat going into latin lover mode, cat-style. "Your smell is sweet like the bins behind the trattoria on roast pig nights, your eyes shine like the scales of a carp jumping out of the water --"

The grey purred. "I'm sure you say that to all the queens."

"No other one has captured me like you do, amore."

Adriana swooned. "Isn't that romantic?"

"He is a smooth talker. Let them have a little privacy."

We moved far enough to be able to watch the cats without eavesdropping on a feline flirtation.

Every girl deserves to spend quality time with an admirer, without an audience hanging onto their words.

The two cats sniffed each other.

Adriana observed the two with an indulgent smile.

I sensed trouble ahead, because I knew that kind of expression.

It started with a trip to a rescue center and ended up with adoptees, plural, once we were back home.

Pirate Cat and his new girlfriend's heads touched as they finished the fish together. They exchanged one last, lingering glance before the big tom jumped up onto a balcony and from there, onto the terracotta roof.

All we needed was a sunset and the sound of violins.

What we got instead was a honking car horn, and a bank of grey clouds. If we wanted to get home in the dry, we had to hurry.

The ride back took longer than I'd hoped, because for once, we were stuck behind an old man in an even older farm truck.

The rain hit us a mile away from our destination. Rivulets ran off my helmet and dripped onto my legs.

In the mirror, I spotted Adriana sticking out her tongue to catch a few raindrops. Just when I was soaked, the downpour stopped.

We watched in awe as a double rainbow was forming over the hills.

It felt like a promise that from now on, there'd be nothing but happiness ahead.

Since there hadn't been a single message for me, or a request to come to the police station, I decided on a long shower first, and then we'd spend the rest of the day on reassuringly mundane things. Chief among them was emailing my mother and Jolene with our interior design decisions.

Jolene received detailed instructions about the dos and don'ts for my workspace. As much as I loved my mother, the idea of giving her loose reins struck fear in my heart.

Her supply of enthusiasm used to be held in check first by my dad and then by financial limits. With a wealthy new husband at her side, I didn't want her to get carried away.

It would break her heart if I came home and had to undo most of her well-meant work.

"Are we done yet?" Adriana gazed out of the windows.

I flung them open. A gauzy haze shrouded the hills and lingered over the rooftops. From around the corner came the mouth-watering aroma of freshly baked pizza.

My eyelids drooped. Adriana snapped her fingers at me. "Are you alright?"

I shook myself. "I'm good. Let me put through an order for dinner, and then we'll have a movie night."

A lasagna later, we settled in with Cary Grant and Katharine Hepburn in *Bringing Up Baby*.

Adriana laughed so hard, she had tears streaking down her cheeks, when a loud knock interrupted the final scene.

"Go away," she yelled.

Another knock came.

"People," she muttered. "Showing no respect."

"Genie?"

I stumbled over my feet as I rushed to the door.

"Come in." Somehow my voice caught in my throat.

Matt hesitated as he saw my pajamas. "Did I wake you?"

"Of course not." I pooh-poohed the very notion that I could be tempted by bed while the sun still stood high in the sky.

He followed me inside, where Cary and Katharine had toppled the dinosaur skeleton. He glanced at the tv screen. "Great movie," he said. "One of the best."

"It is."

"There's something I wanted to tell you." His gaze held mine.

"What is it?" My mind raced back to last night. "Please don't say the police let Paul Stone go and he's after me."

"Heavens, no, you're safe. Beatriz has confessed. She tried to paint herself as the innocent victim who got swept up in her husband's crimes, from what I've heard, but I don't think that'll wash."

"Good. That's a relief."

We both stood there, searching for something to say.

At least I was.

And then I wasn't any longer, because Matt's lips touched mine.

Chapter Twenty-Five

The kiss went on forever.

Matt held me tight to him or maybe I was the one holding him close.

I could no longer tell, until we both had to come up for air and a certain person danced around us.

"Finally. He is one heck of a kisser." Adriana puckered up her lips and made smooching noises.

I kicked her shin. It gave me a short jolt of pleasure, despite the lack of physical impact on her.

"Hey." She pouted.

"Can I just have five minutes of privacy?" I whispered.

"There's nobody here." Matt glanced around to make doubly sure.

"There was a cat on the balcony, staring at us. I'm one hundred percent convinced she understood every single word."

"Cats do," he agreed. "Although I wouldn't consider her an intrusion into our privacy. Unless --" His dark eyes held a specific gleam.

Adriana giggled.

I waved my hand behind my back, signaling her to leave me alone.

There were limits to what I was willing to do or say in her presence - or in Matt's.

Which left me caught between a rock and a hard place. "When are you leaving?" I asked.

"Tonight. I'm due to leave for the airport in less than an hour."

My heart sank. "That soon? I'm staying for another week."

"Right."

"Go on," Adriana hissed in my ear. "Kiss him again, before he thinks you're not interested."

I would have to sit her down for a long talk, once we were alone. To be fair, she couldn't help it that we shared the room. At home, we had more options.

In the meantime, I followed her advice and leaned in for another kiss. This one was even better.

"I can't wait to see you in Cobblewood Cove, Genie Darling," he said after we'd both caught our breath again. "I've never met a woman like you."

Adriana dove in and pecked his cheek. "You sweet, sweet man."

He touched his face. "It sounds crazy, but it's like you change the whole atmosphere around you, in the best possible sense."

Adriana swooned, and so would I have done, if not for a few reservations.

His compliment would have meant more to me if I could have gauged how much was aimed at me and how much it owed to the fact that he really did appear to sense Adriana.

Matt was the only person we'd met so far who experienced a warm, happy glow in her presence.

What if it was in reality she who sparked the jolt of excitement between us, and without her, the attraction would fizzle out?

I pondered that depressing notion as we watched him leave.

Adriana fanned herself. "That was a lulu of a smooch. He is so smitten with you."

A faraway look came into her eyes. She pressed her hands onto her heart.

I had never enquired too much about her love life before she died, to spare her painful memories.

Had she left a sweetheart behind? If so, she hadn't mentioned him.

Could it be that me and Matt were the closest thing she'd had to experiencing a real relationship, if only second-hand? I didn't have the heart to tell her that dating a man with a ghost as my constant chaperone was not my ideal scenario.

We could work on that later.

First, we had more important things to do. At least, more important at the moment. Sorting out the situation with Matt would have to wait until we were home.

I tidied every single item in our hotel room.

Adriana stood on the balcony. Her hands gripped the railing. "How much longer?" Her voice rose in a wail.

I spritzed the air around her with Chanel No. 5.

The scent with its heady mix of roses, bergamot, vanilla and other notes that prevented it from being overly floral, wafted around her. She relaxed, as I'd hoped.

I congratulated myself that I'd purchased the classic fragrance for this special occasion. Adriana had been through enough here in Montepulciano.

Anything that helped her handle her emotions without blowing a fuse, in every meaning of the word, was fine with me.

She still stood there, with a blissful smile and sniffing the perfume her mother used to wear, when the long awaited knock on the door came.

I tripped over myself in my haste to reach the door.

Only a last minute grab of the wall and some assistance from my guardian ghost saved me from landing flat on my face.

Together, we pressed the door handle.

Outside stood Tristan Odell, with a large garment bag over his arm.

"Please come in," I said.

I took the bag from him and put it flat on the bed, with all the care I could muster.

I touched the zipper. "Is it safe to open it?"

"Of course it is." Adriana pulled on the zipper. It moved a little.

Tristan blinked.

"Of course it is," I trilled as I took over the zipper before the poor man decided that his sanity had suffered irreparable damage.

After all, he'd been the main suspect in Paolo's demise, and his auction rooms would need major restoration.

"Isn't it beautiful?" Adriana touched every inch of the little black dress which had finally come home to her.

"You're a miracle worker," I told Tristan. "I was afraid this frock would be held as evidence."

"There was no need, with all the other proof in the room and that confession you'd helped Matt secure." He took my hand and lifted it to his lips. "I owe you more than I could ever repay."

"Don't mention it."

Adriana held out her hand too, either because she also wanted it to be kissed, or because she was making fun of me.

I didn't care.

We had her dress, we'd brought a killer to justice, and we had a promising romance.

No, I told myself, not we.

I had a promising romance.

"How much do I owe you for the dress?" I asked.

"Nothing." His eyes crinkled at the corners.

"I insist." He might feel grateful enough to purchase it for me, but Darlings had never needed charity, nor taken expensive gifts from a man who would need every euro to undo the damage to his palazzo.

"You don't have to pay a single cent," he said. "Neither did I. The family told me to return the dress to you, with all their thanks. It appears the late Lady Taverner wore it to the ball where she met her future husband. Without this very frock she would have stayed in her student digs instead of setting out into society. Your family's donations changed her life."

"That's incredible. Thank you."

"The stories so many objects could tell, eh?" His eyes gleamed with the zeal of a true history fan.

"Indeed," I said.

"Would you care to join me for dinner?"

Adriana gaped at me. "Now he might be carrying a torch for you as well. Too bad for him he's no match for Matt."

It was endearing, if misguided, that she thought it possible that every man would be smitten with me.

He cleared his throat. "That is, Serina has suggested we all meet up to celebrate."

"Is she still around?"

"For a little while."

Did his color change a little? They'd make a great couple, I decided. They both had flair and style, and cared about the same things.

I gazed at my great-great-aunt and her precious dress. "I'd have loved to but I already have other plans."

"I understand." Again, he lifted my hand to his lips and Adriana swooned. "Another evening then, before you leave Italy."

When he was safely gone, Adriana draped herself onto the bed, on top of the Chanel frock.

A few blinks, and I could see her dressed up in it, all understated glamor and elegance.

In the next blink, she was back to normal, in her usual evening gown.

She'd worn that particular garment on the icy night when she'd walked for miles, soaking wet after a fall into the river that might or might not have been caused deliberately. In the end, it had killed her.

"What are our plans for tonight?" she asked. "You don't blow off a fancy meal for nothing and your boyfriend is gone."

I opted for mystery. "It's a surprise. Wait and see."

In keeping with the mood, Adriana insisted on using one of her elbow-length opera gloves as a blindfold for herself when we set out.

Watching her probe the walls as we walked down the stairs and into the hotel car park, made me laugh so loud I had to put down the picnic bag I carried and wipe away tears.

I placed the picnic in the seat compartment of the Vespa, which was this time without the brick.

"Hop on," I told Adriana.

We set off at a leisurely pace. I'd timed it so we would have as little traffic as possible as we headed into the rolling green and golden hills.

Bird song filled the air, and the scent of jasmine mingled with freshly cut grass. The road meandered past dry stone walls, olive groves and young vines.

Once we had left the farm houses behind us and reached the top of a hill, with a view of castles and small towns dotting the landscape like multi-colored jewels, I brought the Vespa to a halt.

"Take off the blindfold," I said. Adriana gasped in delight as she gazed around.

I spread sandwiches and roast chicken breast on a large napkin and opened a small bottle of Prosecco.

"Cheers." I lifted the bottle and waved it under Adriana's nose so she could enjoy a drink, ghost-style.

Since I had to drive back, I'd stick to bottled water.

My great-great-aunt flitted around, a few inches above the ground. It took it as a sure sign she enjoyed herself enormously and that the magic of the Chanel dress had worked.

I had another surprise in store, a playlist I'd agonized over for days. Then we danced.

Luckily the only audience we had as we were jiving and Lindy-hopping and doing the Charleston on a Tuscan hill were a small herd of white cattle grazing while dusk settled in.

Eddie Cantor and Vernon Dalhart crooned.

Ethel Walters and Bessie Smith sang their heart out, and in honor of Cleo at home and our star witness Pirate Cat, I'd added *The Cat's Whiskers* and *The Cat's Pajamas* to the musical selection.

Adriana was twirling and kicking away with unflagging enthusiasm when I sank down onto the grass, underneath a pine tree.

"Whoopee," my great-great-aunt shouted.

I gave her a weak nod, embarrassed by how winded I was. There was no way I could compete with Adriana's boundless energy.

Of course the fact that she tended to take a deep whiff of Prosecco after every song might have something to do with it.

The last notes faded, and with a satisfied chuckle she flung herself on the ground and put her legs over mine.

"This is brilliant," she said. "I wish we could go on and on and on."

"We have a few days left." Thanks to the generous descendants of Lady Taverner, I also had a decent amount of pocket money at my disposal. "What would you like to do? Spend a night in a proper castle, or take a train to Venice and live it up in a swanky hotel?"

"Actually, there's another thing I'd like to do. It's going to be the bee's knees, I promise, so will you please say yes?"

"I might, if it doesn't involve me making a complete fool out of myself in public."

"You never do that."

"Except for the few occasions when you made me talk with you, with other people around."

She crossed her fingers. "It won't happen again, ever."

"Really."

Her eyes grew round. "Don't you trust me?"

Against better judgment I told her that, of course, I did trust her.

I already regretted these words when we drove back to the hotel and I caught her in the side mirrors standing up behind me, waving her arms like a windmill, and singing. "Yes, Sir, that's my Genie, no, Sir, not a weenie."

Still, another Darling trait was that we never went back on our word.

CHAPTER TWENTY-SIX

I had no idea what to expect as I prepared for the task ahead. What had I let myself in for, and what mayhem awaited the poor gelato-makers?

I, or rather we, had enrolled in the class advertised in the gelateria. We were half a dozen students of varying ages and different nationalities, all connected by the love of ice cream and the Italian dolce vita.

We also all wanted to impress Signora Valentino hard enough to become the star pupil and earn the golden ice cream scoop displayed in a showcase. Okay, so it wasn't really gold, and I doubted it could do heavy duty in everyday life, but it was an award.

My gaze kept traveling toward it.

Adriana whispered into my ear.

"Shh," I whispered back, "I need to concentrate."

To my astonishment, it worked. Although she practically hovered over me, Adriana kept quiet while our teacher, a stern grandmother whose instructions where translated into English by her granddaughter, took us through basic knowledge and demonstrated her technique of mixing and stirring and churning, followed by more mixing and more stirring and more churning.

Finally, we were allowed at the bowls.

Adriana sized up the competition by sniffing their concoctions.

She honed in on a bank teller from England who'd confessed to plotting his escape route from the day job via ice cream.

I'd taken to this middle-aged guy. He treated the whole experience as a spiritual connection with his soul and his stomach, something I could agree with.

"He's good." Adriana's fingers twitched. "Maybe I should do something about him."

"No," I hissed out of the corner of my mouth.

To the teacher, I signaled that I'd take a short powder room break.

My great-great-aunt trailed after me. "I want us to win." She pouted.

"Which is fine, if we do it fair and square. If your nose and taste are a great as you say --"

"I can smell the difference between three types of sugar from half a mile away."

"Then you don't have anything to fear. Otherwise, what's so bad if he wins the Golden Scoop? It might brighten up his life."

"And what about me?"

"You have me, and Cleo back home."

The pout vanished. "He does look like a sad old person. You think I should inspire him?"

More likely, she'd give him a heart attack. "Just stick to the plan," I said.

I heard my name being called. "We're ready for the final step."

"Stop lallygagging and hurry," Adriana said. "I know exactly what our gelato needs to be the crème de la crème."

In her excitement, she dashed towards the door and right through it - into the men's rest room.

"Oops." She pulled herself back, laughing. "You don't want to hear what I just saw."

I closed my eyes.

It would be a long, exhausting day, like most of them since my great-great-aunt had popped up in my life. I glanced in the mirror. Any second now there would be grey hair sprouting on my head.

Adriana tugged on my sleeve. "Come on, Miss Dawdle Doodle Dandy. I have no idea how you got things done without me."

I had. Everything had been so much easier - and a lot less fun.

She poked her head through the correct door. "Everybody freeze, champions coming through," she yelled.

Maybe fun wasn't the right word. Where would this craziness end?

A note from Carmen Radtke

Genie and Adriana are back home, and their new gelato-making business keeps them busy.

But when the murder of her friend poisons the atmosphere, Genie and her ghostly sidekick go sleuthing again ...

Read Ghost Stirs The Pot now and join Genie and Adriana in their new fun-filled adventure.

If you enjoyed Ghost Takes A Vacation, please consider leaving a review or a rating! They make all the difference for an author. Thank you!

Cast of characters

Genie Darling, jewelry maker and amateur sleuth

Adriana Darling, her great-great-aunt, a ghost, pet-whisperer, and fellow sleuth

Matt Blake, art and museum security expert

Tristan Odell, auction house owner in Italy

Paolo, security guard

Chiara, his fiancée

Luigi, her belligerent brother

Marisa and Gianluca Galotti, antique store owners

Beatriz and Paul Stone, collectors

Lisa and Fred Schmitt, collectors

Hans and Willem, archaeology students and activists

Serina, beautiful art appraiser

Ettore, retired guard dog and witness
Pirate Cat, another witness
Gigi, Chiara's terrier, character witness

About the
Author

Carmen has spent most of her life with ink on her fingers, cozy crime plots on her mind (thank you, Agatha Christie) and a dangerously high pile of books and newspapers by her side.

She has worked as a newspaper reporter on two continents and always dreamt of becoming a novelist and screenwriter.

When she found herself crouched under her dining table, typing away on a novel between two earthquakes in Christchurch, New Zealand, she realised she was hooked for life.

The shaken but stirring novel made it to the longlist of the Mslexia competition, and her next book and first mystery, The Case Of The Missing Bride, was a finalist in the Malice Domestic competition in a year without a winner. Since then she has penned several more cozy mysteries, including the Jack and Frances series set in the 1930s.

Ghost Takes A Vacation is the second in a series of fun-filled paranormal cozy mysteries.

In real life, Carmen is absolutely law-abiding, has never met a ghost or been able to communicate with pets (sad, but true). The only time she shed blood and swatted a fly was by accident.

Her wanderlust has led her to live in Germany, New Zealand, and the UK. She currently lives in Italy with her human and her four-legged family.

If you want to keep in touch with her and find out more about her work, writing life, and other related things, sign up for her newsletter on her website www.carmen-radtke.com and receive a free quick read!

You can also follow her on Amazon, Book-Bub and Facebook.

Also By

The Genie and Adriana Darling cozy paranormal mysteries
Genie and the Ghost
Ghost Takes A Vacation
Ghost Stirs The Pot
Ghost and the Haunted House

The Jack and Frances cozy 1930s mysteries
A Matter of Love and Death
Murder at the Races
Murder Makes Waves
Death Under Palm Trees
The Mystery of the Christmas Bauble (a novelette)
The Case of the Christmas Angel (a novella)

The Alyssa Chalmers Victorian mysteries
The Case of the Missing Bride
The Prospect of Death
The Tunnels of Doom (coming soon)

The cozy contemporary Eve Holdsworth mysteries
Let Sleeping Murder Lie
A Dash of Deceit
Death at the Dog Show
Murder on the Airwaves

Stand-alone novels
Dig Your Own Grave
Walking in the Shadow